MW01609781

Fighting for Charlotte

ELIZABELLA BAKER

♡/ Elizabella
Baker

No part of this work may be used, stored, reproduced, or transmitted without written permission from the author except for brief quotations for review purposes as permitted by the law.

The characters and events portrayed in this book are fictitious. Any similarity to real persons, living or dead, is coincidental and not intended by the author.

Editor: Raechelle Downing

Proofreader: Judy Zweifel, Judy's Proofreading

Cover design by: LJ, Mayhem Cover Creations

ISBN: 9798770224306

Library of Congress Control Number: 2018675309

Printed in the United States of America

Contents

Chapter 1

April 2022

C harlotte Snyder watched dreamily as her best friend married the love of her life. It may have taken twelve years, and Charlotte had only known him as the elusive ex for most of it, but she couldn't be happier. Leslie deserved that happiness. Especially after those fuckface parents of hers all but ruined her life. Those were two people Charlotte hoped got what they deserved. Karma would be fitting.

Looking past Leslie and Zack, she searched out Brooks, Zack's slightly older brother. The man was devilishly sexy in a tuxedo. She had met and spoken to him only a handful of times, but it took just the first time for her to realize exactly what she wanted; a no-strings-attached booty call from a sexy man in a uniform whenever she came to Texas. And it just so happened that the sexy police officer fits that bill to a T.

When she first met Zack, she had jokingly asked if he had brothers. Turns out, not only did he have them, they were just as equally sexy as Zack. But only one caught her eye. And right now, that man stood not ten feet away and looking abso-fucking-lutely delectable. Which one would think would make her even happier than seeing her best friend get married. But nope, that wasn't the case.

She was regretting the decision to wear a shorter bridesmaids dress. There was no way to discreetly rub her legs together to relieve the ache she felt. Instead, she was forced to stand still. Needing to calm down her libido, she focused on Leslie. Her best friend made for one hell of a beautiful bride.

"You may now kiss the bride," the minister announced needlessly. Zack had already dipped Leslie for a kiss that made even her scandalous ass blush. The crowd hooted and hollered. Feeling the need to look away, she slid her gaze up and crashed into a familiar set of blue eyes. Only this time, they were much darker than she was used to seeing. Almost starving. And if the way his eyes roamed over her body was any indication, he wanted her as his next meal. *Yes, please.*

A shyer woman would have played coy or even blushed from such an obvious look. But she was neither. With equally hungry eyes, she took in every inch of his body. The way his wide shoulders and chest filled out the tuxedo, and the way the pants hugged his ass. From tip to toe and everything in between. Including the enormous erection that she was positive was just for her. Licking her lips, she moved his way as they were set to walk down the aisle together after the bride and groom. Leslie was smart when she partnered them together.

"You keep looking at me that way, hot stuff, and we're going to have one pissed-off Wes when he finds us banging in his house," she panted with a side-eye. Her arm tingled in anticipation from his touch.

"Then I guess we better make sure he doesn't catch us," Brooks replied huskily before dropping her arm and moving through the crowd.

She took one step to follow him but stopped when her best friend announced that it was time for pictures. Tamping down her sexual frustration, she followed the rest of the bridal party to the other side of the lake where the photographer was beginning to arrange family and friends. Charlotte had been to several weddings, so she knew that the next hour would be spent taking a thousand photos. At least some of those photos would be with Brooks. They were the maid of honor and the best man, after all.

"I know that look in your eye," Leslie whispered, suddenly next to her.

"I would sure hope so. I sure as hell ain't hiding the fact that I have every intention of jumping his bones the first chance I get." Charlotte wasn't the type of woman to beat around the bush. Life was too short for that shit.

"Hussy," Leslie laughed. "You've barely spoken to him."

"I'm not looking to be pen pals," she quipped. "More like fuck buddies. I expect his mouth to be too busy to do any type of talking."

"Incorrigible. What am I going to do with you?" Leslie hadn't stopped laughing and the rest of the bridal party was looking at her curiously.

"Love me like you always have. Now enough about my soon-to-be amazing night of sex. Your photographer is beginning to look impatient."

That was all the encouragement Leslie needed to shake her head and walk away to join her new husband. As predicted, they took thousands of photos. Each one was more beautiful than the last. Leslie made a stunning bride, and the love between her and Zack was evident. It was easy to capture it. Unfortunately, the photographer moved things along too quickly for her to get any decent touching in with her sexy partner.

With pictures over, food served, and dancing underway, her role as maid of honor slowed down. Looking through the many faces, she finally spotted the only one she cared for at that moment. Tucked into a dark corner, she saw Brooks staring back at her.

Sauntering that way, she slipped past his parents who were dancing on the makeshift dance floor. She scooted around a very pregnant Leah who, despite how close she was to having the baby, radiated happiness. She sidestepped a giggling Ash, until finally, she stood in the same dark corner as the hot man who made every part of her sing with just a look.

"I was beginning to think I would never get you alone," he teased, cracking a panty-dropping smile. *A fitting term considering what I hope will be happening soon.*

With a smirk, she stood on her tippy-toes and whispered in his ear, "The devil himself couldn't keep me away from what I hope is going to be one hell of a fantastic orgasm."

"Oh, you'll get more than one," he promised.

Grabbing her hand, he pulled her farther away from the reception. She followed willingly, which just proved that she was, in fact, the hussy Leslie called her. Not that she cared. She was simply after a good time. Tomorrow she would be on a flight back to Boston with only her memories to keep her warm at night. That and the occasional egotistical asshole she met at the bar who barely knew how to use the dick he was given let alone pleasure anyone else with it.

He stopped when they were a few feet into the woods. Spinning her around, he pinned her to a tree, giving her only a moment to register the tough bark on her bare shoulders before he crashed his lips to hers. He pulled her head back, demanding she open her mouth for him, something she was all too willing to do. As tongues dueled, she barely had time to catch her breath before he was shifting gears. With his lips no longer on hers, he kissed and nibbled his way down her throat, her collarbone, and alongside her boobs, continuing the trail until he was on his knees in front of her with his hands tracing up and down the outside of her legs. The man didn't waste any time

"I want to taste you. That fantastic orgasm you wanted? The first one will come while my mouth is between your legs," he breathed against the front of her already wet panties, and her dress already bunched in his hand at her hip.

"Fuck yes," she panted.

Reaching back, she grabbed the trunk of the tree as he lifted one of her legs over his shoulder. He pushed her panties to the side, and she threw her head back when she felt his tongue lick her slick folds.

"Sweet. So fucking sweet. Like honey," he breathed.

His cold breath contrasted her heated sex. Her ass scratched against the bark as she rocked her hips forward and back, shamelessly riding his face. Thrusting her hand into his hair, she tugged at the roots. She was probably causing him pain, but he didn't seem to care as he continued to devour her until the climax slammed through her. She avoided screaming as she bit down on her lip, throwing her head back against the tree again. She was going to give herself a concussion at this rate.

Slowly dropping her leg, Brooks stood up to his full height of six one. With the pad of his thumb, he wiped her juices from his lip and stuck it in his mouth.

"You tasted just as I thought you would," he growled near her ear.

The gesture had her ready for more. Slipping beneath his arm, she spun him around until it was his ass against the tree.

"My turn," she whispered as she dropped onto her knees on the forest floor. Unzipping his pants, she pulled out his already straining cock, as Brooks gasped. His tip was wet, so she used her thumb to circle the head. She licked her lips and looked up to meet his eyes as she slowly flicked out her tongue, getting her first taste of his salty goodness.

"Fucking A," he groaned, his hand flying to the back of her head to fist her hair and encourage her on. Not that she needed any encouragement. She wanted his cock in her mouth just as much as he did.

Using her lips on his head to tease him, she drew him in inch by slow inch until he hit the back of her throat. Circling with her tongue, she repeated the torturous process a few more times until the hand cupping the back of her head pulled on her hair.

"Fuuuuck," Brooks swore, "suck me harder."

The huskiness in his voice spurred her on. Sucking harder, she added her hand to match her tempo, while her other hand squeezed his balls.

"I'm going to come," he said as he attempted to pull her back, but she refused. "If you don't want me spilling down your fucking throat, move back now," he groaned. Again, she ignored him. Instead, she increased her tempo until the hand gripping her hair was almost painful and he growled out his release, shooting straight down her throat.

When he finally slowed down, she leaned back licking her lips once again, sucking in every last drop. The lust in his eyes was all she needed to know he had fully enjoyed their time in the woods. Standing up, she took a few steps back and turned on her heels while he continued to catch his breath.

"See you around, hot stuff," she threw over her shoulder as she fixed her dress and sauntered off, a smirk on her face.

Chapter 2

B rooks sat at the kitchen island the morning after his brother's wedding to his high school sweetheart. It had taken him a while to get used to calling her Leslie rather than Lauren, but after Zack explained what happened, he understood her wanting to keep the new name. It was a tragedy really. He never particularly liked her parents but that didn't mean he thought them capable of assisting human traffickers. When Zack had described what they had done, or at least what they were suspected of doing since the case was still open, he had been shocked. As a police officer, he hoped they got the book thrown at them in the end. As her brother-in-law, he wanted to murder the sons of a bitches. Not just for her but for all those people whose lives they ruined.

"You must be getting old, brother. You left the wedding awfully early. Unless it was a certain red-haired hottie that stole you away," Garrett laughed as he joined him in the kitchen.

Charlotte's hair was more blonde with red in it than actually red but he wasn't about to tell Garrett that. His mind flashed back to that particular green-eyed siren who rocked his world in the woods and then proceeded to just walk away. He had been so stunned that rather than following her back to the wedding and looking like a lovesick fool, he had gone straight back to the house his family was using for the weekend.

"Didn't want the hangover," he lied. "Seems you didn't mind so much. You look like shit, by the way." He attempted to take the conversation away from himself. His brother's eyes were bloodshot, and his hair was sticking up in all directions. He was squinting and it looked like he had just rolled out of bed and thrown on a pair of shorts before trudging to the kitchen.

Garrett threw him the middle finger while he opened the refrigerator and grabbed the carton of orange juice. Foregoing a glass, he chugged from the carton.

"Gross!" their sister Alexa yelled when she entered. Taking the carton from Garrett's hand, she didn't seem the least bit concerned as the orange juice dribbled down their brother's chin.

"What the fuck, sis? I was drinking that," he whined.

"Yeah, and now whatever diseases your man-whoring ass has are all over it," she tossed back.

"I'm the man whore?" he yelped. "What about Brooks? He's the one who ran off with some chick last night."

So much for keeping the conversation away from his activities. He gave his brother a "what the fuck" look before turning an innocent smile over to his baby sister. As the youngest of the six of them, she was the wild one. They often joked that their parents were too tired at that point to properly discipline her. Alexa was the most outspoken of them all. She cursed like a sailor and told everyone exactly what she thought. Just like another female he wanted to get to know.

"I just wanted a peaceful night of rest and to not be hungover this morning," he added innocently.

"Peaceful, my ass. I know you better than that," she tossed over her shoulder as she walked back out of the kitchen with a granola bar in her hand. She didn't even bother to pretend she wanted to talk to them.

Grabbing an apple from the bowl on the island, he whipped it at his brother. Garrett was certainly still hungover because the former baseball star's reflexes couldn't catch it before it hit him square in the chest.

"Dude, what the fuck was that for?" Garrett whined again while he rubbed the area the apple hit. It was becoming clear that a hungover Garrett equaled a whiny bitch. Who would have thought?

"Way to throw my ass under the bus."

"How did Garrett throw your ass under the bus?" Rhett asked as he joined them.

Rhett was the youngest of the boys and only a year older than Alexa. He had followed in Zack's footsteps and joined the Army. He was still enlisted, and they were lucky he was granted leave to come home for the wedding. Truthfully, up until a couple of days ago, they were sure he wasn't coming. He'd surprised them all when he showed up.

Brooks grumbled "nothing" under his breath at the same time Garrett said, "Brooks definitely fucked Charlotte last night," with a shit-eating grin on his face.

There was no way he was keeping Charlotte out of any of these conversations. Sighing, he resigned himself to the fact that his family was a bunch of busybodies who needed to know everything that was going on in each other's lives.

"Leslie's hot best friend?" Rhett's eyebrows shot up in surprise.

"Yup." Garrett dramatically popped the P. "The one and the same."

"Score." Rhett punched him in the shoulder.

"I never said that. I just came back early so I wasn't hungover like the rest of you," he grumbled. That was his story and he was sticking to it. He would rather his family bust on him for getting old than because Charlotte dropped his ass after getting exactly what they both wanted.

"If you say so, man, but I gotta say, I would have totally tapped that if I had the chance."

Grabbing another apple, he whipped this one at Rhett for the comment. "Don't talk about her like that. Mama raised us better. Not to mention she's too damn old for you."

"She's not that much older," Rhett grumbled.

"Brooksy's got it bad," Garrett barked out. Using their childhood name for him as they laughed uncontrollably.

"Real mature, the two of you," he grumbled again. He should have let it go. Instead, his comment only added fuel to the fire.

"In all seriousness," Garrett asked, elbows now on the counter and his chin resting in his hands, "is she as feisty in bed as she comes off? I mean, considering the red hair and all."

It was like they were back in high school. Talking about the popular girls that they knew were way out of their league.

Brooks flashed back to last night. The way her thigh had pressed into his shoulder as he feasted on her. His hair still hurt from the way she pulled on it as her climax took over. Then the way she flipped him around and dropped to her knees to suck him off had him getting hard again. Not that it had gone down much since she walked away. He was beginning to think he would forever be in a semi-hard state every time he thought about her.

"More so by the look on his face," Rhett added in with a devilish smirk.

He threw them both the middle finger as he pushed off the stool and left the kitchen, their laughter following him out. He was barely paying attention when he ran straight into Lucy on the way out.

"She totally blew you off, didn't she?" his sister stated, matter-of-factly.

"Eavesdropping," he countered.

"Not hard to do when you all talk so damn loud." She shrugged. "Plus, I saw the way Charlotte looked after she came back. At first, I would have guessed smug, but as the night went on, I got the feeling it was more sadness when she realized you hadn't returned."

Hope blossomed in his chest at his sister's words. There was a huge part of him that hoped Charlotte didn't just leave without a goodbye, but he couldn't get that look she wore as she sauntered off out of his head. He had been basking in the afterglow when she had burst his bubble with a simple "see you around."

"Truth?" he asked.

"We used to tell each other everything," she replied a bit sadly. Her eyes shifting to the ground.

It was true. As the two oldest, they had always shared secrets. It didn't matter that she was his older sister. There were times when he had asked her embarrassing questions as a teenager so he didn't fuck up with a girl. And he had gladly threatened any guy who so much as looked at her the wrong way. But that had changed after she got married. Now they barely spoke, and when they did, it was mostly about work. She didn't speak about her love life and never asked about his. Until now.

"We didn't have sex, but we did fool around. And then she walked off without so much as a goodbye."

"Ah." She smiled. "So *she* was the one to do the walking away instead of you and that has left you with mixed feelings."

The smirk on Lucy's face aggravated him. Although it didn't reach her eyes like it used to. She used to tease him that one day he would find his match. He wasn't prepared to admit it but he was afraid she might have been right. He wasn't exactly a player like his other brothers. He dated, but never for more than a couple of weeks, and he was always the one to walk away as soon as it started getting serious.

Grumbling, he forced out an "I guess so."

Lucy just chuckled as she patted him on the shoulder. "Call Zack. Make sure he and Leslie aren't having any problems starting their honeymoon and maybe casually ask if Charlotte flew back to Boston. If so, then forget she exists, or man up and go after the woman."

With that final parting shot, his sister moved into the kitchen and joined Garrett and Rhett at the kitchen island where they were shoveling their faces with food.

Making his way through the house, he thought about what Lucy said. Was he having mixed feelings? Would she have affected him so much if he was the one to walk away? He wasn't sure but he did know that he wasn't about to call his brother on his honeymoon and beg for information. He would give it until they came back. Hopefully, he would get her off his mind in the meantime. With that decision settled, he grabbed his gym bag and headed out to get a workout.

Chapter 3

Charlotte stepped off the plane in Boston. Since Leslie left for her honeymoon that morning, there was no reason to stay in Texas any longer. The plan was always to leave the morning after and she had done just that. What happened with Brooks last night didn't change anything. She had a career and a life in Boston, neither of which she was ready to give up for a man, no matter how many truly amazing orgasms he gave her. Just the thought of him had her rubbing her legs together.

Rolling her luggage out of the airport, she hailed a cab. She had only been in Texas for a few days but, as was usual for her, she had overpacked. When Zack had picked her up at the airport and saw the two large rolling suitcases plus a carry-on, he had laughed his head off. Now she watched as the cab driver threw her heavy, overstuffed bags in the trunk before she climbed in. She should feel bad about how much she packed, but she didn't. One never knew what a girl was going to need.

She was about halfway to her apartment when her phone rang. Looking down at the screen she chuckled when she saw "Badass Author Bitch" pop up. Her best friend couldn't even go one day without calling her.

"You're supposed to be on your honeymoon," she said in lieu of hello.

"I am. Zack is currently checking us in and I just happened to check to see if your flight landed. When I saw it did, I figured I would call and let you know we arrived as well."

She was calling bullshit on that. She didn't need to see her friend's face to know she was a shitty liar. It was in her voice. And as any true friend would, she called her out on it.

"Uh-huh. I'm not buying it. Why did you really call?" She could probably guess but she was going to make Leslie say it. She was a bitch like that.

She loved her best friend. For the past twelve years, they were inseparable, ever since meeting their senior year of high school. They even lived in the same apartment building until Leslie reconnected with Zack. Now Leslie lived in Texas, but they spoke every day. Sometimes multiples times a day and visited when they could. Which was usually when her best friend came back up to visit, or when she needed to go down for wedding stuff. Which was more often than she originally imagined.

"Okay, fine. I saw you go off with Brooks. The two of you were gone for a while, and then besides a quick goodbye, I didn't see you again all night."

Well, that wasn't entirely true. She had stayed at the reception but had purposely avoided Leslie and Zack in hopes they didn't figure out what happened in the woods.

"Did you spend the night with him?"

"I don't kiss and tell."

"Bullshit. Yes, you do. All the time actually. Now spill."

She should have seen that coming a mile away. It was a blatant lie and she wasn't any better at lying than Leslie was. She had hoped her best friend would be too distracted by her new husband to notice. She was going to have to text Zack and let him know what an awful job he was doing if his wife had time to gossip.

"Okay, so maybe I did sneak off with Brooks, but I didn't spend the night with him." There. That's all she was going to say on the matter.

"Why the hell not? All you've talked about since meeting him is how hot he is!"

A very true statement when she thought about it. What had started as a joke soon turned into a conquest; to see if the man was half as good as he looked. Turned out, he was even better which was exactly why she had to walk away. Men like that stole women's hearts. She wasn't about to let that happen.

"He *is* hot but that doesn't mean I want to start something long distance." Okay, so maybe she wasn't done talking. Damn her best friend.

"Who says it needs to be long distance? You keep saying how much you miss me. Move to Texas already."

"I like my life here, and I love my job. I'm not ready to give all that up yet," she tried to protest.

Although the thought had occurred more often the longer they were apart. She missed her best friend more than she cared to admit. Even to Leslie. But that didn't mean she wanted to make a rash decision that would uproot her life. Especially not if there was a man involved. That was a recipe for disaster.

"Fine, but one of these days you're going to cave and then I'm going to be so excited. I miss you."

The sound of Leslie's voice cracking nearly did her in. She needed to change the subject and fast.

"I miss you too, but you're on your honeymoon, which means I don't want to hear from you unless you need to hide a body. Then I'm your girl."

"Why would I need to hide a body on my honeymoon?!" Leslie asked with exasperation.

"Exactly! So don't call me. Enjoy and have fun. Have lots of sex. Practice your baby-making skills and all that. You deserve it. I love you. Bye."

Before Leslie could argue, Charlotte ended the call. Resting her head back, she let out a long sigh. That was a close one. Luckily for her, Leslie was easily distracted and wouldn't chance calling her back a second time. Zack would likely not be happy to be sharing her for long. It was their honeymoon after all.

"You know you got a good friend when they are willing to help you bury the body," her cab driver said with a smirk in the rearview mirror.

Not sure what to say in return, she let out a nervous chuckle. It was a good thing they were just pulling up to her apartment building. Otherwise, she would have been concerned that the cab driver had an alternative meaning. *Get yourself together. You read too damn many crime novels. Time to go back to romance.*

She quickly tipped the driver as the doorman took her suitcases inside for her. She was fortunate to have found a place with excellent security and super sweet doormen around the clock.

"Thank you, George," she said as he placed her bags in the elevator for her. George was her favorite doorman. He had been there before she moved in and always joked that he would be bored if he retired. Which was why at seventy years old he continued to work, but now only part-time. He said he spent the rest of his time fishing in the harbor. He was the epitome of what she envisioned a grandfather would look and act like. Like the Hallmark version at Christmastime.

Getting off the elevator, she slowly made her way to her door. Letting herself in, she dropped her keys and bags just inside the entry. She wasn't in the mood to unpack, so instead, she trudged into the kitchen, grabbed a glass of wine, and flopped on her couch.

Her apartment wasn't large, but it suited her just fine. As a single woman living in a big city, she only had a few requirements. The place had to have some security and be new enough that things didn't need to be fixed every other month. Her place fit that nicely. The downside, however, was that it cost her a pretty penny. She was one of the lucky ones with an inheritance. Although she had long since stopped relying on that. Now she did pretty well for herself working for one of the top fashion designers in the world.

Sipping her wine, she thought back to the night before.

Had she made a mistake when she walked away from Brooks last night? She refused to let a man be the reason she changed her life, and it wasn't like Brooks was the first man she walked away from after screwing around. In fact, she always walked away first. Usually, because the men she picked were self-centered pricks who only wanted to hear how great they were. And usually, they weren't great at all.

They always got themselves off and left her high and dry. But not Brooks, he had gotten her off with just his tongue. And in return, she had made sure she reciprocated by sucking him dry. It had been one hell of a night and the best she had in God only knew how long.

Unfortunately, that still didn't change the fact that she wasn't ready for anything other than sex. She refused to let her heart get involved and Brooks was the type of man she would easily fall in love with.

No, she did the right thing. It was better for both of them that she just walked away. Except, then, why did she feel so bad?

Chapter 4

It was lunchtime, not that it meant anything when one was a police officer. There were no scheduled lunch breaks. They simply just stopped to eat when they could and where they could. Right now, that was a sub shop in the heart of Austin with one of his favorite partners.

"This moodiness is getting ridiculous. I never thought I would say this but you're worse than my girlfriends. So I'll tell you the same thing I tell them. Either call her and demand to know what the fuck is going on, or forget about her," Officer Sky finished with a nonchalant shrug.

He and Abigail Sky had gone through the academy together. Every now and then they were fortunate enough to be working the same shift in the same district. Today was one of those days, but Brooks was beginning to think it wasn't so great.

"She just walked away and flew back to Boston with zero communication. Pretty sure she made her intentions very clear," he huffed.

"Then go with door number two and forget about her."

Eyes squinted, he shot her a dirty look. One she returned with a giggle. He should probably take her advice, but he was like an addict. One hit just wasn't enough. He wanted more. That, or what Lucy said was true and he was only obsessed because Charlotte had walked away. Either way, a week away hadn't done anything to diminish his wanting.

"Not helpful," he grumbled.

Abigail continued to chuckle as she took another bite of her meatball sub.

"So what would you like to do instead?" she asked innocently, but he knew better. She had no problem making fun of him.

He had no idea. He should just forget about her but that was proving to be impossible. He had woken up almost every morning fisting himself after he dreamed about her. It was getting old. He tried going to a bar, but it was no use. Not a single girl caught his attention.

"I don't have a clue." He sounded pathetic even to his ears.

"Have you been preparing for the SWAT test?" she asked.

Oh good, she took pity on him and changed the subject. Shifting gears, he thought about the career change he was considering. After seven years on patrol, he was finally taking the plunge. He had been eligible to take the test for three years, but each time, he couldn't commit. He never felt ready or as if he had learned enough.

"Yeah, I feel pretty confident about the physical test and the firearms course. I've been working hard on the endurance part whenever I can. But as we both know, it all comes down to the oral board."

It was a well-known fact in the Austin Police Department that SWAT took their applicants seriously. It didn't matter if he aced every physical and firearm test. If the board felt he wasn't a good fit, then he didn't stand a chance. And there was no way to prep for it either. It wasn't like he sat there while they asked him questions. No, it was much more in-depth. The oral board would speak to his fellow officers and supervisors. They would ask about his dedication and hard work, was he trustworthy or not, and a million other things he couldn't even begin to list. It was stressful, to say the least.

"You got this!" Abigail encouraged. "You were made for SWAT. I've been telling you that since the academy and nothing you say is going to change my mind."

He laughed at her response. He could always count on her no-bullshit attitude to kick his ass into gear. And she never disappointed. He never thought he would have a female best friend but that was exactly what Abby was. They had tried the whole "going out" thing once, right after the academy, but it only took ten minutes into their "date" for the two of them to realize their relationship was more brother and sister than romantic. She reminded him a lot of Alexa with her carefree, go-with-the-flow attitude and sailor's mouth.

His thoughts were interrupted by the squelch of his radio: "Henry 203." Throwing the rest of his sandwich away, he answered his radio and prepared to continue his shift. His short lunch was over.

After a few more calls and towards the end of his shift, he finally caved and called Zack to see how he and Leslie were doing now that they were back from their honeymoon.

"Took you long enough to call, asshole," Zack answered on the second ring.

He looked at the phone to make sure he had called the right person. With a shake of his head, he put the phone back up to his ear.

"Why the fuck would I call you on your honeymoon, dick?"

His family used insults as endearments. To most outsiders it probably sounded harsh, but it was just the way they were. Their professions probably had something to do with it.

"To ask about Charlotte. Now I lost a fucking bet to my wife because you took too damn long."

Counting to ten in his head, Brooks tried to remember why he finally went against his own advice and called his obnoxious brother. Oh, that's right, because he couldn't get a certain woman out of his head.

"You always lose when you bet. You're the worst gambler I have ever met and that's saying a lot in my profession," he threw back.

It was no secret Zack couldn't win a bet to save his life. Not against his brothers, and from what Brooks heard, not against his teammates either. Betting against Zack was a sure-fire way to make a little extra cash. Not that the asshole ever paid up.

"Doesn't matter. It still took you over a week to call and ask about her."

"Who says that's why I'm calling?" He sounded defensive but he couldn't stop it. First Abigail and now Zack. Everyone was all of a sudden concerned with his love life.

Leslie's *tsking* was like a gunshot in his ear. "Dude, do you have me on fucking speakerphone?"

Great, now it wasn't just Zack but Leslie as well who was going to harass him about Charlotte. Although, as her best friend, Leslie might have some of the information he was trying so hard to deny he wanted.

"Of course, he does," Leslie gloated. "Especially when it involves my best friend."

He didn't have to see her to know she wore a smug look. He just wasn't sure if it was because she won a bet against her husband or because she had information Brooks wanted. It was probably a little bit of both.

"Traitor," he grumbled, eliciting a chuckle from both his brother and his wife. "And since you brought it up, how is your best friend?" he grudgingly asked. He avoided saying her name in hopes of not sounding too desperate. Who was he kidding? There was no way anyone would believe that right now.

"I thought you would never ask," Leslie started sarcastically. "Now, I'm not one to break girl code, but I'll make an exception since you're family. Charlotte hasn't outright said it or anything, but I know she's missing you. She's just too damn stubborn to admit it."

He thought about what Leslie said. Hope bloomed but crashed just as quickly. Leslie might know Charlotte better than anyone else, but that didn't mean she knew what her best friend was thinking. And since Charlotte didn't actually admit it to the one person she shared everything with, maybe it wasn't true.

"Stubborn is a good description," he laughed dryly.

"Don't write her off just yet," Leslie replied. Gone was all hint of laughter or sarcasm. "She's good at pushing men away. What she needs is someone who is going to fight for her."

His mind blanked at the raw advice. Unable to form a response, he just grunted.

"I'm serious." She did sound serious, so he agreed. He needed time to think about this. Did he want to fight for her? Or did he just want more sex? He was in uncharted territory, and he didn't know what to think, about anything.

The subject was quickly changed to how the honeymoon went and the plans they were making. They had purchased a fixer-upper before the wedding and were still in the process of turning it into their dream home.

Zack told him a little bit about his current assignment. They were protecting a woman and two young girls who had escaped a human trafficking ring. All discussion of Charlotte had ended and a part of him was relieved. He kept going back to what Lucy said. Maybe the only reason he was hung up on her was that she had been the one to walk away.

After he hung up with Zack, he finished out his shift and was just jumping into his truck to leave when a text message came through.

LESLIE: just in case you wanted to just stop in or call

The next message was Charlotte's contact information including address and phone number. He laughed at the name Leslie used for Charlotte's information: Not Just a Booty Call. He continued to laugh as he saved the information to his phone and tossed it on the passenger seat before heading home. His sister-in-law might have just made up his mind for him. Maybe he would make a surprise visit after all.

Chapter 5

As she climbed out of the taxi, Charlotte pulled down her skintight black dress. She leaned through the passenger window and paid the driver before he sped off. With a huff, she looked at the line to get into the underground club, asking herself for the millionth time that night why the hell she agreed to go out when she could have been home curled up with a book.

Instead, she had let Michelle, her much younger co-worker, convince her that a Saturday night out would be great. Apparently, this was the hottest club in Boston. The old Charlotte would have been all over it, but recently the thought of getting dressed up and hanging out with douchebag frat boys or wannabe sleazeballs in cheap suits no longer held the same appeal.

"Charlotte!" Michelle squealed from her place in line. "Over here." She dramatically waved.

Rolling her eyes, but plastering a fake smile on her face, she waved back. "Hey, girly," she said with too much emphasis as she joined Michelle in line.

Michelle must not have noticed because she immediately started rambling. "OMG, I'm so glad you decided to come out. Isn't this place epic? It's all anyone is talking about right now. Anyone who is anyone has shown their face in here!"

It might be true for those who were just above legal age or trying to impress someone, but neither applied to her anymore. At almost thirty, standing in lines to enter a hyped-up club didn't have the same appeal it used to.

Charlotte wasn't able to get a word in, so she just continued to nod her head and smile. It took them almost an hour of standing in line before they finally made it inside. Tossing the bouncer a flirty smile, she stepped into the obnoxiously lit room. She wasn't sure if the owners were trying to attempt a modern sheik vibe with all the gray and chrome, but the colors bouncing off reminded her too much of a neon bowling alley. Looking down at her pale skin, the lights had her looking like she swallowed a glow stick. *Fan-fucking-tastic.*

"It's even better in person!" Michelle squealed.

That was certainly debatable. She was about to make up some lame excuse to bail when Michelle giggled as a guy wrapped his arm around her middle, effectively pulling her co-worker out onto the dance floor. With a slight wave, Charlotte was left to her own devices. Not wanting to be rude without saying goodbye, she sulked over to the bar and hopped up on a barstool. With her feet dangling, she met the eyes of one of the bartenders.

"You look like you could use a shot," the bartender commented as she pulled a shot glass from the rack below the bar.

The woman was petite with black hair in a pixie cut. The tips were an electric blue. Her boobs poured out of the half top that seemed to be the customary uniform in the place. That, paired with the Daisy Dukes, and this was every man's wet dream. She probably made a killing off them in the place.

"You would be right," she yelled over the music. "How about a Three Wise Men? Since I doubt I'm going to find that in the human form this evening."

The bartender shook her head with a chuckle as she pulled the three whiskey bottles from their slots. Pouring not just one but two shot glasses, she slid the first one toward Charlotte before picking up her own.

"Here's to the best Jack, Jim, and Johnnie you will ever meet. Cheers!"

They both downed the shots. Shaking her head, Charlotte marveled at the way the whiskey warmed her insides on the way down. Most of the time she stuck to social norms and ordered some type of girly drink, but tonight wasn't one of those nights. She had no intention of getting wasted, so she would limit her amount of shots, but that didn't mean she couldn't have a few to chase away the man who had been consuming her thoughts lately.

"So what brings you in tonight?" the bartender asked.

"A co-worker convinced me it would be a good idea. Ten minutes into our hour wait outside I realized she was wrong but didn't have the heart to bail on her."

Being a bitch and bailing normally wouldn't have bothered her, but she had been in a funk lately. It started when Leslie left and only got worse after the wedding. She suspected a certain hot cop had something to do with it but refused to look at that too closely.

"Ah, and where is your co-worker now?"

Waving a hand in the general direction of the dance floor, Charlotte answered, "Out there somewhere. She bailed on me when some dude pulled her out to dance."

It was ironic really. She hadn't wanted to be the one to bail and leave Michelle by herself in some new club, but clearly, Michelle didn't have the same moral code. Leslie would never have left her alone. She knew how important the girl code was. Just the thought of her had Charlotte wishing she was back home curled up on her couch. As much as she hated to admit it, she really missed her best friend.

"Well, hello kitten. Where have you been hiding all my life?"

With a side-eye, she took in the man who had plopped onto the stool next to her. Man was probably the wrong term since the boy barely looked to be out of high school, let alone old enough to be in a club.

"Nope," was all she said before once again meeting the eyes of the bartender as she wiped down the bar just a few feet away. With a nod, the pixie lady began pouring another shot.

"Oh, come on. Give me a chance. A cougar like you must be looking to pick up a young stud like myself."

Turning her head ever so slowly, she watched as the bartender stifled a laugh behind her rag just as she slid the shot her way. Never taking her eyes off the boy, Charlotte tossed the shot back, slammed the glass down, and wiped her lips with the back of her hand before opening her mouth. Screw ladylike. The boy had effectively brought out the bitchy side she had been missing.

"Cougar? Do I look that fucking old or are you just that fucking young? Did you need your mama to drop you off tonight? Boy, I'm not even thirty yet. Get the hell out of here."

"Bitch," he grumbled before sliding off the stool and heading back to the dance floor.

Taking in a long cleansing breath, she turned back to the pixie bartender whose name she should really learn because the name Pixie was probably rude. Although that's exactly who she reminded Charlotte of. No longer needing to control her laugh in front of the customer, Pixie doubled over with tears in her eyes.

"Damn, I thought for sure you were going to knock that kid on his ass, and I was going to have to convince my boss it was an accident."

Charlotte chuckled at the response. It was probably pretty close to accurate. For a moment there she considered if spending the night in a jail cell was worth it. The only reason she decided against it was because the only person who could bail her out lived in Texas. *Damn you, Leslie. I need the Carrie to my Miranda.*

"I'm Charlotte, by the way, since I might need you as an alibi if this night keeps up."

"Tina." The woman shot her hand out and gave a gentle shake. "And no worries. I got your back if the police come calling." With a wink, she moved on to help another customer further down the bar.

Charlotte spun around on the stool and looked at the crowd. For the first time in her life, she felt past her prime.

Hardly anyone in the place looked old enough to be out drinking. Most of the guys looked like frat boys or gym rats who spent more time staring at themselves in the mirror than actually socializing. It was sickening because not too long ago she would have easily hooked up with any of these boys for a quickie. Not because she was interested but because she knew they would run away the moment they finished and that was exactly what she preferred. At least she thought so until a certain Lynch brother ruined her. Now every guy she looked at was being unfairly compared.

She no longer caring about being rude, so she threw some cash down on the bar, waved to Tina, and headed out of the club. Flagging down the first taxi she could find, she crawled in and gave the driver her address, as she leaned her head back against the seat. She was just starting to nod off when the taxi came to an abrupt stop. Looking out the window, she recognized her own building. She handed over some cash and climbed out. The door was barely closed before the driver was speeding off.

With a wave to the night doorman, she took the elevator up to her apartment. She tossed her keys and purse, kicked off her shoes, and hurried to her bedroom to change. It took all of one minute for her to ditch her club outfit and pull on a pair of comfy pajama bottoms and a sweatshirt. Finding her most recent book boyfriend, she padded her way back out to the couch to curl up and read. There was nothing better than a good book and absolutely nothing beat a book boyfriend. No human man could compete. Well, maybe there was one man.

Chapter 6

He stepped out of the taxi in front of Charlotte's apartment building. He had called Leslie when he landed to make sure Charlotte would be home. He had lucked out that she had the day off. He had wanted to take an early morning flight, but his sister-in-law had warned him that Charlotte wasn't a morning person and wouldn't respond well to being woken up. So instead, he took a later flight and hoped she didn't have plans to go out. It would really suck if she had a date or something. Leslie had reminded him it was a Sunday and ensured him that wasn't the case, but still.

He knew her building had security, so he waited at the front desk until they called to make sure he could go up. When the woman behind the desk gave him the all-clear to access the elevator, he let out a breath he hadn't realized he had been holding.

Okay, she didn't tell you to fuck off and deny you entry. That was a good start.

At least he hoped so. As he rode the elevator up to her floor, he wiped his sweaty palms against his jeans. Either he was more nervous than he thought, or the elevator was stiflingly hot. He didn't get the chance to debate it any further before the door clicked open. Stepping out into the hall, he noticed Charlotte was standing in her doorway waiting for him.

This was the first time he'd seen her in anything other than heels or some girly outfit. If he thought dolled-up Charlotte was sexy, it was nothing compared to her raw look. Her face didn't have a trace of makeup, hair was thrown up in what Alexa called a messy bun. She had on the cutest pair of pajama bottoms with snowflakes and a huge sweatshirt that hung off one of her shoulders. He was tempted to nibble on that shoulder, but based on the fire burning in her eyes, she probably wouldn't welcome the gesture.

"Leslie broke the girl code," she hissed as she stepped back into the apartment and waved him in.

With one sweep of the place, he took in the small but tidy apartment. The kitchen looked modern, and the living room was inviting. He could see the door he assumed led to her bedroom.

"Who says Leslie told me where you lived? I have my own ways of finding out where people live," he challenged. He wasn't about to get his sister-in-law in trouble. He actually really liked her.

"Pretty sure it's illegal to use your job to find some chick's address," she threw back. Damn, she was cute when she was spitting mad.

"Touché. But I plead the fifth on how I got your information." He shrugged nonchalantly. Even though he felt anything but inside. His stomach hadn't stopped flipping around since the elevator doors opened and he saw her waiting for him.

"The least the bitch could have done was give me some warning so I had the chance to make myself look even semi-presentable," she added with a humph.

Moving quickly before she stormed off, he leaned in and whispered, "I prefer this side of you."

He watched as a shiver ran up her body and left goose bumps in its wake. *So she is just as affected by this as I am. Good to know.*

A shock traveled through his body as she placed her hands on his shoulders. Pushing him back, she challenged, "So you prefer a slob."

Crossing his arms over his chest, he took another step back before responding, "No, I prefer real. Not a Barbie wannabe. I didn't say there was anything wrong with getting dolled up every now and then, but a woman is a hell of a lot sexier when you see the natural side of them."

"Natural, like, hairy legs and armpits?" Fuck, she loved to argue. And for some reason, it turned him on. That was new. He could have sworn he preferred the quiet type.

"Woman, do you plan to argue with everything I say?" he asked with exasperation.

"You're the one who showed up unexpectedly to my place. If you don't like my smart mouth, you can leave." She pointed toward the door.

"I can think of a lot of other things you could be doing with that mouth," he mumbled under his breath.

If looks could kill, he would be dead at that moment. Her eyes might as well have been a gun pointed directly at his forehead. She showed no mercy as she stomped his way, hands on her hips.

"If you want my mouth around your cock, just say so, hotshot." She punctuated each word by jabbing a finger into his chest. Grabbing her wrist, he spun her around so that her ass was cradled against his growing erection. With her arms pinned in his, he leaned over and nibbled just behind her ear.

"As much as I loved your hot mouth around my dick, I would prefer to be buried deep inside you the next time I come."

She groaned at his words, her ass rubbing against his crotch. Shifting both of her hands into his one, he used his free hand to trace a line down her covered belly and across the top of her pajama bottoms. Pulling back the elastic, he flattened his palm low on her belly, just inches from her opening.

"Hmmm, no panties. What a naughty girl," he growled into her neck.

"I rarely wear them," she panted.

Just the thought that she went out in public without them had him almost bursting. He bit the side of his cheek to stop from embarrassing himself and dipped his finger into her dripping center.

"You're so fucking wet. Does the thought of my dick turn you on?"

"Yes." She continued to pant as he pumped first one finger, then two. He palmed her sex, increasing the pace as she clung to him.

"Not yet," he growled. "You finish when I tell you to."

She whimpered as he pulled his hand from her pussy. "Don't worry, this is going to be a quick fuck. It's been too long."

He shoved her pajama bottoms down as she leaned onto the counter, her whole body shaking from being on the edge of release. He unzipped his pants and pulled his straining dick free to slide on the condom he'd brought just in case. Pushing her legs as far apart as her pants would allow, he bent his knees and lined himself up with her opening. Slamming all the way into her, she yelped at the sudden intrusion. He wrapped his arm around her stomach to keep her to him and laid his head against her back, taking a moment so he didn't finish before they even got started.

"Fuck me," Charlotte groaned. Her head was thrown back as she pushed her ass out more to take all of him. He couldn't deny her request.

"You feel so fucking good."

That was an understatement. Sliding into her was like heaven. The way her walls clenched onto his dick pulling him in as if they were made for each other. He could spend all day inside her warmth.

Pulling almost all the way out, he slammed back in again and again. Each time she let out another moan. He was so damn close, he needed her with him.

Using his thumb, he massaged her nub. When he felt her walls begin to quake, he growled into her ear, "Now. Come for me now, beautiful."

As if her body had waited for his command, she convulsed around his dick, screaming his name. With one final thrust, he joined her, as he too screamed her name and pulled her tighter, letting his orgasm explode inside him.

It was several minutes before he felt confident enough that their legs could hold them before he slid out of her hot core. He instantly missed the warmth. Standing up straight, he tucked himself back into his pants.

"Where's the bathroom so I can dispose of this?" he asked as he pointed down to his still half-hard dick.

"Second door on the right." She pointed without looking his way.

He wasn't sure what to make of it but that would have to wait until he cleaned himself up. It wasn't like she was going to hightail it again. This was her place after all. Finding the right door, he stepped inside and placed the condom inside a tissue before throwing it in her trash. Making his way over to the sink to wash his hands, he grabbed the edge and just looked at himself in the mirror.

This wasn't the plan, asshole. The entire flight, he had repeatedly told himself he wasn't going to just have sex with her. The plan was to discuss what happened at the wedding and see where they wanted to take things. The last thing he needed was to be distracted by mind-blowing sex against her kitchen counter. Giving himself another pep talk, he finished washing his hands before going back out to join her.

He found Charlotte sitting at the small kitchen table, her one knee bent up on the seat with her head resting on it. She looked so innocent. Opposite of the woman who just minutes ago was begging him to fuck her. Something she absolutely didn't need to do since it's all he had been thinking about since the last time he saw her. *Get your mind off sex already, dumbass.*

"Why did you fly all the way out here, Brooks?" she asked the moment they locked eyes.

"To talk," he answered honestly.

"You could have called if that's all you wanted."

"Would you have answered?" he shot back quickly.

Her only response was to shrug her shoulders. It was what he expected and feared. There were numerous times that he pulled up her number to either call or text. But each time a little voice in his head convinced him she would probably just ignore it. Based on her non-answer, that little voice was probably right.

"So, what now?" she asked.

"Now we talk. Like we should have done when I first arrived but got distracted instead."

He wasn't about to regret the distraction. He had woken up almost every morning thinking about what it would feel like to be inside her. Now that he knew, it was probably going to be worse. Before, he could only imagine, but now his body knew what the real thing felt like. He was screwed.

"I'm not looking for anything," she whispered.

Those five words were like a shot straight to his heart. He had never been in love, but the way his heart was breaking right now, he wasn't sure he ever wanted to be. The sadness in her eyes only made it worse. *I guess that answered the internal questions of if she was looking for more.*

"Friendship is the best I can offer at the moment. I'm not ready for anything more. Especially not something long distance. I'm sorry."

What was he supposed to say to that? He didn't really have any defense. She was right. He had no idea how they would make long distance work. He was never inclined to try with anyone before. Of course, now that he was even slightly considering it, the woman he wanted was emotionally unavailable. So that left him with two options; he could head back to Austin and forget what happened or he could accept the friendship. At least it was better than nothing at all.

"Friend zone it is," he chuckled. She gave him a weak smile in return.

The rest of the night was spent with a light dinner and a movie. They sat together on the couch but no cuddling or touching was involved. It was like the moment they agreed to friendship, all chemistry flew out the window. At least for her. He, on the other hand, spent the entire night half-hard and willing his dick to stop. She offered him her couch for the night since he had to catch a flight first thing in the morning. He wasn't really in the mood to find a place to stay so late in the evening, so he took her up on her offer. And after a restless night of sleeping, he snuck out in the morning with a simple note and caught a flight back home.

Chapter 7

Charlotte slept like shit. How she was expected to get a good night's rest after a mind-blowing orgasm, followed by an awkward evening, was beyond her. But she had no one to blame but herself. She was the one to suggest the friendship. She just didn't expect him to agree so easily. She had hoped for at least a little argument. Although, given how the first argument ended, maybe that wasn't such a good idea. *I mean what kind of relationship would it be if every argument ended in sex?* Probably a pretty good one now that she thought about it.

And who knew she would like a man who took charge? The way he told her when she could come had been so damn hot that she had spent all last night reliving it over and over in her head. So much so that several times she had almost stormed out and demanded he did it again. But that would defeat the purpose of friendship only.

So instead, she had a restless sleep and stayed in bed even though she had been awake when he left that morning. She couldn't face him just yet. When she was sure he was gone, she padded her way out to the kitchen to make some coffee.

She was certainly going to need the pick-me-up today. Setting her mug on the counter, she noticed a piece of paper neatly folded with her name on it. She reached over and, with shaking hands, unfolded the note.

Charlotte,

I really enjoyed our evening together. Here is my number, text me sometime or call if you ever need anything. I'd love to just talk and get to know the amazing person Leslie is always talking about.

Your friend,

Brooks

She crushed the note to her chest. Her vision blurred with unshed tears. Why did he have to be so sweet? It was almost worse. She had assumed he would go back to Texas and completely forget she existed. Yet here he was handing out an olive branch. She looked at the clock. He would be in the air in thirty minutes. She would send a quick text once she was sure there was no chance he would text back and then she would hide away with one of her book boyfriends. She had a to-be-read list a mile long that she could easily sink into to distract herself until she had to be at work. With that thought in mind, she headed toward the bathroom to wash away all thoughts of Brooks.

It was exactly thirty minutes later when she sent him a text.

Charlotte: I'm assuming Leslie gave you my number. Have a safe flight and let me know when you land safely.

She saved his number in her phone under Big Dick BFF. Chuckling to herself, she set the phone on the counter in the same spot she had been bent over just last night. She wouldn't be able to look at the spot without thinking about the way he slammed into her, stretching and filling her in the best ways possible. She was surprised when her phone beeped just a moment later.

Big Dick BFF: Will do :)

Charlotte: Aren't you supposed to be in the air? How are you responding?

Big Dick BFF: The airplane has Wi-Fi

She smacked herself on the forehead. *Duh, dumbass.* It was the twenty-first century after all.

Charlotte: Right. Well, fly safe

Big Dick BFF: ;)

The phone suddenly started ringing in her hand and had her nearly dropping it on the counter. Seeing it was Leslie, she sighed in relief until she remembered it was her supposed best friend that gave her address to the hunky police officer she had just been talking to.

"You traitorous bitch," she answered after a few rings. "What the fuck happened to the girl code, huh?"

Leslie's chuckling in her ear had Charlotte contemplating just how much she really missed her friend, or if she could live with the fact that she wanted to murder the meddling woman.

"So, you didn't have a good night? Good to know," Leslie replied sarcastically.

"I said no such thing and don't change the subject. What happened to warning a girl? I mean, I opened the door in my snowflake pajama bottoms."

"The white and silver fuzzy ones? I love those! And they are super adorable on you."

"I know, right?" she squealed. "Hey, wait. That's not the point. The three of you totally ambushed me."

"Three of us?" Leslie asked, confusion in her voice.

"Yes, three. I know damn well your husband isn't innocent in any of this," she grumbled.

Ever since her best friend reunited with her high school sweetheart, they were inseparable and told each other everything. Which would include meddling into her love life.

"Hey, now," she could hear Zack shout from somewhere in the background, followed by a grunt. It was most likely Leslie had just hit him for not keeping quiet.

"I knew it!" She pumped her fist in the air triumphantly until she realized there was no one in the apartment with her to see it. Slowly, she brought her fist down awkwardly. If someone were a fly on the wall at the moment, they would think there was something mentally wrong with her. *They wouldn't be wrong.*

"Okay, fine, I admit it. I may have convinced Brooks to fly out and it might have been me who gave him your address, but you can't tell me it wasn't worth it."

She said nothing. She didn't want to admit Leslie was right. She couldn't remember the last time she had such good sex. The boys she had been meeting lately were worthless, and if she were honest, her sex drive had been lacking. Which was ironic considering how much she had picked on Leslie about her lack of a sex life right before she reunited with Zack. Now it was her turn to crack out Bob as her new go-to. *Yeah, since you just friend-zoned the only good dick you've had in forever.*

"I'm pleading the fifth." Her words reminded her of Brooks last night. He had said something similar.

"Oh no, you don't. Dish or I'm calling Brooks and asking him to tell me what happened," Leslie threatened.

She would do it, too. She didn't make threats lightly. Charlotte should know, she taught her best friend everything she knew. The only person she could blame in this situation was herself.

"Fine, but Zack needs to leave the room. It's too weird having him listen in while I talk about his brother's cock," she yelled loud enough in hopes that Zack would hear what she was saying.

"I'm out! I don't want to hear another fucking word," he shouted back.

She and Leslie laughed as she heard Zack grumbling about not needing to know anything about his brother's dick or where he stuck the fucking thing.

"Okay, he's gone. Spill, bitch, and don't leave out a single detail!"

"Girl! I only have one word. WOW!" she started.

She explained everything from the moment she received the call from the front desk, how they argued, how the argument turned into hot angry sex. Angry sex that included him pinning her against her counter and having his way with her. How she wasn't allowed to come until he allowed it.

"Wait, he really said that? Holy-fucking-hell that's hot, and just might be used in a future book."

Oops, sorry, Brooks. She probably should have censored that part, but it was too hot not to dish about. Brooks knew what Leslie did for a living. And her best friend didn't keep it a secret that she used people in her life for inspiration.

Brooks should be honored. At least, that's what she was going with if the discussion ever came up.

"Yup." She popped the P. "It really was hot. I never thought I would dig a commanding guy but I would absolutely let him do more dirty things to me if it means he growls at me like that again."

"So...does that mean you're going to keep seeing each other?" Leslie asked.

She took a deep breath before she answered, knowing Leslie was going to flip her lid once she explained the rest of the night.

"Not exactly." She winced. "I told him I couldn't do more than a friendship right now."

"What! Like what the actual fuck does that even mean?! I love you, but if I were standing in front of you right now, I would slap you upside the head!"

This was exactly what she expected. Grumbling, she responded, "I freaked out. I didn't want to do long distance and I sure as hell didn't want to be some booty call, so I said the first thing that popped into my head. Friendship only. And you know what really sucks?"

"What's that?" Leslie asked, concern in her voice.

"He agreed. After mind-blowing angry sex, he agreed to just a friendship. We spent the rest of the night eating dinner and watching a movie, and not once did he try anything. He even slept on my couch like a gentleman and slipped out before I got up this morning. He left me a note, saying he enjoyed our time and hoped to continue talking as friends," she rushed out in one long breath.

"Ouch," was the only response Leslie had.

Plopping down on the couch, she was exhausted. So far she had spent the conversation either pacing or leaning against the counter. Her legs no longer supported her.

"Did I fuck up that badly?" she asked in a whisper.

What she wouldn't give to have her very best friend sitting with her now, sipping a glass of wine as they had this conversation. Why did Leslie have to move away?

"No, sweetie, you didn't fuck up," Leslie soothed. "The fact that he wants to continue talking means you weren't just a booty call, and he hasn't given up. You just need to give it some time. Maybe it's a good thing you're going to go the friends route first. Take the time to get to know each other. That way if you ever wanted more, you would already know more about him."

She sighed at the logic. It made sense and, given that she wasn't prepared for anything long term, it was probably better they parted the way they did. Hopefully, her heart wouldn't get involved and she wouldn't get hurt.

With renewed energy, they talked for another thirty minutes, including a little about what had been happening with the team and Kyle's new woman and kids. She was happy to know that Kyle had possibly found someone. She had recognized the loneliness in the man's eyes even if he would never admit it.

Then Leslie explained some new ideas she had for another series. It was still in the planning stages, so they used the time to bounce ideas off each other. As a reader, it was Charlotte's favorite thing to do. She loved helping with ideas and then reading about how Leslie turned them into amazing stories. There was something magical about knowing she had a hand in the creation process.

It was several hours later, while she was at work, when Brooks finally texted her.

Big Dick BFF: I've landed safely. I hope you're having a great day

Charlotte: I'm glad to hear that and it's not bad. A slow day at work, so I'm enjoying the calm while it lasts.

She worked for a high-end designer. It was rare that they had walk-ins off the street. Most of the clients were celebrities or housewives of super-rich dudes. Her boss had, for the most part, an appointment-only policy but occasionally someone would call that they were in town and would be stopping in soon. Today wasn't one of those days and she was in between clients at the moment.

Big Dick BFF: Well, I hope it stays that way for you. Would it be okay if I called you after you got off work? Just to say hi.

She bit on her thumbnail. Would it be okay? And what did it mean? She usually wasn't one to overthink stuff like this. Frustrated with herself, she sent off a response before she changed her mind.

Charlotte: Absolutely! I'd love that. I'll let you know once I'm home.

Big Dick BFF: Okay, cool. Talk to you later.

She placed the phone to her chest with a sigh. *What have I gotten myself into?*

Chapter 8

Charlotte: Absolutely! I'd love that. I'll let you know once I'm home.

Brooks: Okay cool. Talk to you later.

He leaned his head against the headrest of his truck. He had texted her as he was walking to the parking lot after landing, but he wasn't sure if she would answer or not. He had no idea what to expect with the whole friendship thing. The only female friend he had was Abigail and that was simply platonic. There were zero feelings on his end. That wasn't the case with Charlotte. The only way he was going to survive this friendship was if he put all those feelings into a box and slammed the lid shut. Easier said than done. It was a good thing she was halfway across the country.

He drove back to his house in a fog. A year ago, he had decided he was sick of living in an apartment with too many nosy neighbors who constantly thought that he could solve every one of their little problems just because he was a police officer. So he bought a little Cape Cod on the outskirts of the city. Most of his neighbors were newlyweds who were just starting families. The biggest problem he ran into was kids running through his yard. And that didn't bother him at all. He much preferred to see kids outside playing than stuck in front of video games.

He waved to his neighbors as he drove through the cul-de-sac and pulled into his driveway. He hunched into his seat and just looked at his house for a few minutes. He hadn't thought much about his future when he purchased the place. He hadn't been in any type of relationship, so there was no one's opinion he needed to ask. The only thing he had even looked at was the crime rate for the area. His realtor had even joked that he was the easiest client she had ever worked for. He had only looked at two other houses before deciding on this one.

Now he wondered what Charlotte would think about it. Did she prefer the simple life of the suburbs or was her preference to live in a big city like Boston with all its hustle and bustle? From what he had gathered from Leslie, the two had lived in the same apartment complex ever since moving out of Charlotte's parents' house. It was just one of the many things he planned to learn about her.

Realizing he had spent far too long just sitting in his driveway, he turned off the ignition and headed into the house. When he had made the rash decision to fly to Boston, he'd brought nothing along but a small backpack with a change of clothes, a toothbrush, and deodorant. He had freshened up as much as he could that morning before hopping on a plane, but he felt gross. The first thing on his agenda was a shower.

Standing under the pulsing showerhead, he thought back to the previous night in Charlotte's kitchen. The way she looked bent over the counter as he demanded she wait to come until he gave her permission. He rarely let women see that side of him. More often than not he tamed down his urges, but for some reason with Charlotte he wanted to see if she would fight him. To see if she would let him take control. And when her body obeyed, it was as if he had found his other half.

The thoughts alone had him growing hard. Leaning his head against the wall, he pulled on his dick, pumping to the memories of her moaning his name and the way her ass looked slapping against him. It didn't take long to feel the familiar tingle in his toes, and then in his dick, with the pressure building and his breathing heavy, before he exploded down the tiled wall.

He relished in the aftershocks, now picturing Charlotte's face and the way she looked with her head resting on her propped-up knee. Clinging to the image, he reached for his two in one, and quickly washed, before jumping back out of the shower just minutes after he originally went in.

It was hours later, after cleaning, re-cleaning, using his home gym, pacing, using the gym some more before his phone finally beeped.

Charlotte: I'm home. Just going to grab a quick shower and then I can call you if that's ok

Not even waiting five seconds, he had the phone open and his thumbs were flying across the screen.

Brooks: Hey! Sure, yeah, that would be great

Smooth, asshole. Nothing like letting her know how desperate you are and the fact that you have spent all afternoon waiting to hear from her. So much for shoving his feelings in a damn box and slamming the lid. If he didn't get himself under control, he was going to lose the little ground he had gained.

Ten minutes later his phone rang. Fumbling to hit the answer button, he finally got it right after the fourth ring.

"Hey, hi. Wow, that was quick," he said with a nervous chuckle.

"Hi yourself," she chuckled as well. "My after-work showers are usually quick. It's the morning ones that I stand in until the water turns to ice before I finally climb out."

"Good to know. So how was work?"

He knew nothing about what she did. He remembered Leslie mentioning that she worked retail but that was all. He wasn't sure what kind of retail.

"One of my appointments was cranky. There wasn't a single thing I showed her that she liked. She's usually super picky anyway but today was over the top. The rest weren't bad. One of my new clients was splurging, so it was three hours of nonstop trying stuff on. She took almost everything I recommended, so that was good."

"I know I'm just a simple man, but I thought you worked in retail?" He had no idea what clients or appointments had to do with retail. As far as he knew, a person walked into a store, looked around, and purchased what they wanted. End of story.

She laughed and answered, "I guess retail is one way to put it. I actually work for a high-end fashion designer. Everything she makes is one of a kind. So clients book appointments in advance, and when they come in, they try on what was designed for them or picked specifically for them. Often times the designer will make a bunch of items just because and those are what we provide for walk-ins. It's very exclusive. Most of my time is spent following the trends and helping tailor that to our clients."

Wow, that was the opposite of what he thought she did. No wonder she always looked so put together. Her entire wardrobe was probably custom-made for her.

"Okay, that makes more sense. I was confused there when you first starting talking about clients and appointments."

"Yeah, I wouldn't really call it a boutique or store. The only reason my boss hired me is that she has zero people skills. She is great at designing clothes, but she pisses off more clients than she keeps. I'm more like the go-between. It works better that way."

"Do you like it?" He was curious. A lot of people he met picked a career because it paid well or they thought it was their dream job but it turned out it really wasn't. It was rare to find someone who was passionate about their job.

"Absolutely. I love fashion. So, to be able to spend my entire time working when really, all I'm doing is tracking the latest fashion is a dream come true. It makes me happy when my clients like what I have chosen for them or my boss asks my opinion on a new design she's considering. The only thing that sucks is when clients are cranky like the one I had today. I'm pretty sure it's her life's mission to be as difficult as possible, but I'm determined to crack her. I feel like once I break through that shell, a whole new world is going to open up."

The excitement in her voice when she spoke about her job made him smile. Never had he heard someone talk so passionately about what they did for a living. It now made sense as to why she hadn't moved when Leslie did. Despite how inseparable they might have been, Charlotte had something she loved even more in Boston. That realization wiped his smile away. There was no way she would ever consider dating a man who lived so far away. Not if a move was something that would ever need to be considered. For either of them.

"So you get to meet celebrities and such? That must be exciting." He brought his thoughts back to the conversation.

"Sorta. Most clients require me to sign an NDA, so I don't get to talk about it with anyone. Plus, my boss has a rule in my contract that even those clients who don't have one, still fall under the same rules. Basically, I can't discuss my clients at all. Which sucked every time I wanted to tell Leslie who I got to meet that day," she answered, her voice dripping with disappointment.

"But enough about me. What did you do today?" she asked with renewed energy.

"It was my day off, so basically I spent the day lounging around my house." That was sort of true. He spent the day in but he wouldn't necessarily call cleaning an already clean house lounging. More like a nervous habit.

"So, video games and binge eating?" she chuckled.

He could listen to her laugh all day. Each time she did sent his stomach tumbling like the teacups ride at the fair.

"No video games. I don't own any gaming systems. More like, cleaning and working out."

"Ah, you're one of those guys. Spends all his time at the gym checking themselves out in the mirror."

That had him throwing his head back and roaring with laughter. He knew the kind of guys she was referring to. It was the reason he had a home gym and rarely went to the one in town. Occasionally, he would use the one at the station if he wanted a particular machine he didn't have, but even there the guys spent more time bullshitting than actually working out.

"I'm not sure if I should be offended that you think I'm so into myself, or flattered that you noticed I work out." He continued to laugh so hard there were tears in his eyes.

"Oh, I noticed you work out. I just wasn't sure if it was because you're a peacock or genuinely care about your body," she stated simply.

"A peacock," he roared with laughter again.

"Yeah, you know. A guy who acts outlandish just..."

"I know what a peacock is," he interrupted, barely able to talk from laughing so hard. "I'm just surprised that's the term you came up with."

"It's pretty much the very definition of every guy I have met in the past couple of years."

That sobered him up. He didn't think there was anything that could stop the rolling laughter he had just experienced. He was wrong apparently.

"I can assure you it's not the peacock reason and I'm not even sure I would say it's because I care about my body since I eat like garbage most of the time. I work out because it's expected that, in my line of work, I keep myself in shape. Plus, I'm considering taking the SWAT test and the physical tests for that are pretty tough."

"Good to know," she answered. He wasn't sure what to make of her tone. She almost sounded relieved but there was something else. Sadness maybe. He couldn't quite put his finger on it, and without actually seeing her face, he couldn't read her.

"So what do you normally do in the evenings after work?" he asked. *Please don't say go out with guys.* He repeated in his head over and over again.

"I spend time with my numerous book boyfriends."

"Book boyfriends?" *What the fuck was that?*

"Yes." She dragged out the word. "I love to read. Sometimes it's a murder mystery but oftentimes it's romance. There is just something about the men in those books." She sighed.

Ah, she liked romance. He was putting that in the memory vault for future reference.

"So these book boyfriends, what is it about them that keeps your interest?" Was he fishing? Absolutely. Did he care? Absolutely not.

"Oh, you know, the tough alpha type," she answered casually. "Always out to save the girl. Strong, handsome, confident, nice muscles and ass. But a total marshmallow at heart when it comes to a woman. Being funny is a huge perk. The kind who gets all caveman, throwing the woman over his shoulder and growling 'mine.' Those kinds of book boyfriends."

He was stunned silent for a moment. He wasn't the type of guy who read books nor did he compare himself to other men, but he was just a bit jealous of these fictitious men Charlotte was clearly in love with. Lucky them.

"Did I lose you?" she chuckled.

"Nope, just trying to figure out where the authors come up with inspiration for these so-called men," he grumbled.

"Well, your sister-in-law used your brother and his teammates for inspiration not too long ago," she casually threw out.

Of course, she did. He was going to have to have a serious talk with Leslie and Zack about this whole "book boyfriend" thing. How the fuck was a man to compete with that?

"I bet she did," he mumbled.

"Don't be jealous she didn't pick you to write about." She laughed hysterically in his ear. As the laughter wound down, she said, "As much as I would love to keep up this banter, I'm exhausted and ready to crash."

It bummed him out that she was tired. He hadn't gotten his fill of her yet. He should have been just as tired. He hadn't slept well, spent most of his morning flying and the rest of the day pacing. He should have been ready to crash as well, but he was the opposite. Talking to Charlotte renewed his energy

"Okay, goodnight, beautiful. Sleep well."

"Goodnight, hot stuff."

It was several minutes after she hung up before he was finally able to put the phone down. *I'm fucked. Royally fucked.* There was absolutely no way he was going to be able to keep up a friendship-only relationship. His heart was already involved and there wasn't a damn thing he could do about it.

Chapter 9

Charlotte lay in bed the next morning thinking about her conversation with Brooks the night before. She'd never had a male friend. That was probably sexist, but every guy she had met had only one thing on his mind: to get into her pants. Not that Brooks was any different; actually, he had already been in her pants, and yet he still agreed to be only friends. Nearly two thousand miles separated them and the man wanted to text and talk on the phone. She had no idea what to do with that. Except maybe follow along and see how it went.

Ugh! What the fuck did I get myself into?

The surprising part about it all was that she actually enjoyed talking to him. She thought he was funny, and when he had asked her to describe her perfect book boyfriend, she had nearly died. Mostly because it took all of two point five seconds for her to realize she had been describing him to a T. Hopefully, he didn't realize it. Otherwise, she was more screwed than she realized. And not in the physical sense either. Although, there was no denying the man knew how to screw her brains out.

Argh! She grabbed one of the dozen pillows on her bed and smashed it into her face. *Maybe I can just smother myself. I don't work today, so no one would find me for a bit.*

That was a lie. Leslie was sure to call or text at some point, so there was no way her best friend wouldn't sound the alarm if she chose not to answer. With a sigh, she removed the pillow and pushed herself off the bed. She was being a bit dramatic, and if it were Leslie acting the same way, she would have kicked her ass. It was probably a good thing Leslie no longer lived in the same building. She wouldn't have been able to get away with moping around.

Dragging herself into the shower, she took an extra-long time under the pounding water. She finally got out when she heard her phone dinging from the bedroom, indicating a text message. Knowing if she didn't answer soon, the phone was bound to start ringing, she wrapped a towel around herself and padded back to the bed.

She was surprised to see the text wasn't from Leslie after all.

Big Dick BFF: Good morning, beautiful. I hope you slept well.

A grin broke out from ear to ear. Unlocking the screen, she quickly typed back.

Charlotte: Morning, hot stuff. I did! And how about you? Sleep well or too busy dreaming about me?

She hit send before her mind fully registered what she sent. Frantically trying to think of something funny to counteract it, she stopped when the little bubbles appeared. Holding her breath, she waited not so patiently until the bubbles disappeared. They reappeared before disappearing again. It happened two more times and she was about to type "never mind" in all caps when his response finally came through.

Big Dick BFF: Dreaming about you would be the same as sleeping well for me

She had no idea what he meant by that. Did that mean he did dream about her? Did he actually sleep well? She was so confused, but there was no way to ask without sounding desperate. Which would be the opposite of the friends-only relationship that she had asked for. *Idiot!*

Charlotte: I'll take that as a compliment :). Are you working today?

She was proud of herself for sounding relaxed when the truth was her stomach was currently on the tilt-a-whirl at an amusement park, and if she didn't get off soon, she was likely to hurl.

Big Dick BFF: Yeah, but not until tonight. I'm on night shift all this week.

Charlotte: That's a bummer. Is it hard switching from nights to days? My sleep schedule would be all messed up and I would probably be a bear lol.

Understatement of the year. It was no secret she liked to sleep. Or that if she didn't get it, someone was likely to die. She made it pretty well known, actually.

Big Dick BFF: You get used to it. It has taken a few years but I'm finally on a pretty consistent schedule.

Charlotte: That's good, I guess. Is it quieter at night?

Big Dick BFF: It's bad luck to say the word quiet lol. Usually, once someone opens their mouth, it means we get our asses handed to us.

Charlotte: Oops. My bad

Well, she hoped she hadn't cursed him. She should probably have known that little tidbit from the book she just read but she just thought it was an urban myth. Guess not.

Big Dick BFF: That's ok. You're still my favorite friend ;)

The winking face always did her in. She wasn't sure what it was about when a man used it that made her swoon. Actually, it was only one man. And she was currently in a text conversation with him.

Charlotte: Favorite or only?

She added a thinking and silly face afterward. She was surprised at how easy it was to talk to him. Looking down she realized she was still wrapped up in her towel, her hair dripping wet. She had been so caught up in the exchange that she had forgotten she was hopping out of the shower when her phone had gone off. Taking the phone with her to the bathroom, she towel-dried her hair while she waited for him to respond.

It was several minutes later before he finally responded.

Big Dick BFF: Favorite

The blushing face after the one word was all it took. She was a goner. Despite not wanting a long-distance relationship, she had a sinking feeling she wasn't coming out of this without a broken heart. Needing to step away for a bit, she didn't respond. Reaching for her blow dryer, she took the time to thoroughly dry her hair. Most days she would just take the dampness out and call it a day, but right now, she needed to keep busy. Otherwise, she was going to overanalyze the entire conversation.

It was just some harmless flirting. At least that's what she kept trying to convince herself. It was fine as long as she kept her heart out of it, kept any feelings she had locked up tighter than a chastity belt.

She jumped, banging her knee on the door handle of her bathroom vanity when her phone rang. Scrambling to answer, she didn't look to see who was calling before answering with a breathless hello.

"Am I interrupting something?" Leslie chuckled from the other end.

"Shit. No. I was blow-drying my hair when the ringing startled me, so I banged my damn knee off the drawer. Hurts like a bitch," she complained.

"Mhmm. So it wasn't because you have a certain hunk on your mind or anything?"

Was it illegal to try to murder your best friend? I could probably convince the police officer it was justified. She contemplated how she could possibly get away with that when what Leslie said sank in.

"Does your husband know you're calling his brother a hunk?"

"Who said I was talking about Brooks?"

Well, shit. So much for playing things cool. The first rule in covert operations: don't ask a question to which you don't already know the person's answer. Reason number fifty she would make a shitty spy. Scratch that off the "if I ever lose my job and need to find a new career" list.

"You haven't shut up about me and Brooks since your wedding. So it's safe to assume that's who you were talking about." She tried to save herself.

"I noticed you didn't deny it though."

Her friend was relentless, like a damn dog with a bone. If she didn't give her something, there was no way the conversation would ever move past talking about a certain hunk.

"Okay, fine. Maybe I was thinking about your husband's brother because he was texting me," she confessed.

"Wait, the two of you are texting!?" Leslie screeched. "When the hell did that start? Is it like texting, texting, or sexting? If so, you better dish."

I really suck at this whole spy shit. UGH.

Charlotte slapped a hand to her forehead. And when did Leslie become so vocal? Hell, she had been trying for years to get the damn woman to open up. A few months with some badass military men and suddenly she wasn't afraid to say what was on her mind. She was so proud.

"Just texting. It's all very vanilla right now, so nothing to report. Sorry to disappoint you."

"I'm not sure I believe you, but I'll let it go for now."

"Gee, thanks."

Leslie couldn't see the eye roll she just gave her. Too bad, because it was a good one too. A full-facial-expression one that couldn't be missed.

"What are besties for?" Leslie chuckled.

"Support. Love. Affection. To cry big fat alligator tears with while eating ice cream straight from the container," she tossed out. "Not to laugh at, pick on, or make fun of," she finished with a humph.

"Since when?" This time it wasn't a simple chuckle Leslie let out. No, her damn best friend had the audacity to laugh so hard she snorted and then laughed even harder.

Note to self: look for a new best friend ASAP. She was putting out a listing as soon as the conversation was over. Maybe the pixie bartender from the other night would be interested. What was her name? She thought for a minute before snapping her fingers when it came to her. Tina! That was the chick's name. Maybe Tina would be interested in being her new best friend since her current one sucked.

It was a solid minute before Leslie had herself under control enough that she could finally get another word in.

"I feel like you've learned just a little too much from me," Charlotte started, "and I'm not sure I like it anymore."

"Yes, you do. Who are you kidding?"

"Okay, you're right, but seriously...where did my shy and hidden best friend go? Move a girl to Texas and suddenly she changes."

She wished she was there to witness the change. Since the moment they met, the only thing she had wanted from her friend was to see her stop hiding and flourish. Now that it was finally happening, she was bummed she was too far away to be a part of it.

"All good changes I hope?" Suddenly Leslie sounded unsure.

"Yes, all good. I just hate that I'm missing it."

"Well, you could always move down. Then you wouldn't be missing it. And I would get my best friend back plus a bunch of new ones. You have already met the other women and loved them. Think of all the fun we could have together."

Heaven help Texas if that was the case. Those other women Leslie spoke about weren't just those attached to Zack's teammates. Oh no. It was their crazy friends as well. Ash herself was crazy but add in Monica and Trista and havoc was sure to follow. With all of them together, the state wouldn't know what to do, and neither would Wes, Zack's semi-stuck-up and mean boss.

"Maybe Texas isn't looking so bad after all," Charlotte teased before adding, "But not yet."

"Way to burst my bubble," Leslie all but whined in her ear.

"I'm not saying it will never happen," she laughed. "The chances have improved since we last discussed it, so take the little win and shut it."

"I'm going to hold you to that." Charlotte heard a muffled discussion in the background before Leslie spoke again. "Hey, I have to go but this conversation isn't over. I want to hear more about that vanilla texting later."

"I keep telling you I don't kiss and tell. Say hi to Zack for me and get on making me an aunt already!"

"Not yet! Sheesh. You and Zack are relentless. Goodbye, I'm hanging up now."

She chuckled again when the line went dead. She should have thought to use that earlier to distract Leslie. She had only been joking, but it would appear the two lovebirds were already discussing plans to make the little Lynch family that much bigger. She needed to remember that for future reference when she needed a subject change from Brooks.

Then it hit her. If Leslie did, in fact, get pregnant, would she be okay being a long-distant aunt? *Hell no.* She would want to spoil and cuddle that baby every chance she got. It just might be the one thing that would convince her to leave behind good ole Boston and head south. Hopefully, Leslie was effectively distracting Zack, and it wouldn't be a reality soon.

With thoughts of babies and cuddling on her mind, she went out to the kitchen to decide what she wanted to make for breakfast. It was past time she got herself motivated for the day. Starting the day talking to Brooks had thrown her off and now she wasn't sure which way was up or down.

Chapter 10

"How many times are you going to look at your phone? Does my company suck that much?" Abby asked.

They were working the same shift again, so as usual, they were grabbing lunch. He had thought he was being discreet every time he looked to see if Charlotte had messaged him back yet. Apparently, that wasn't the case.

"Sorry, wasn't trying to be rude," he apologized.

"So you going to tell me why your eyes are glued to your phone or just pretend like I didn't ask?" She laughed at him.

With a sigh, he responded, "I texted Charlotte this morning and haven't heard back yet."

"Is that unusual for her?"

All laughter in Abby's voice was gone and replaced with concern. She was a police officer after all. Just like him, her mind probably went straight to did something happen to the woman. He would have as well if the roles were reversed.

But he had other information which was why he wasn't sure how to respond to that. For the past two weeks, everything had been going great. He and Charlotte texted every day and spoke on the phone several times a week. For the most part, the conversations were light and just a bit flirty. Nothing too deep or meaningful. At least until last night. Somehow the conversation had turned to marriage and babies.

Apparently, his brother and sister-in-law were going to start trying to have a kid. From what he gathered, Zack was pestering Leslie for babies and Leslie was patiently explaining that, until he was the one growing the kid, he could wait until she felt she was ready. Brooks wasn't entirely sure how the conversation went since he was getting the information secondhand from Charlotte but he knew his brother. The man could be impatient when he wanted to be.

"A little. We talked last night and it got a little awkward before she hung up but I usually at least get a *good morning* back."

Charlotte had gone silent when he had confessed that he did in fact want the whole marriage-and-kids life, and that he could see himself with a bunch of children running around. He was one of six kids, all of whom were close. With three brothers and two sisters, his house was always loud and full of life. He wanted that for his future children. He wasn't sure if Charlotte disagreed or not, but shortly after that, she claimed she was tired and wanted to get some rest. Then radio silence.

"Maybe she's just busy, or over your boring ass," Abby chuckled.

Well, he sure hoped that wasn't the case. He was just finally getting used to the whole friendship thing. They had a light banter going that he looked forward to each day. He thought it would be harder to keep his feelings bottled up, but it turned out it was easier to text or talk. He wasn't so sure he could have done the same thing if they were living in the same state. He was bound to want to touch or hold her if he saw her in person, but on the phone, she didn't seem to mind when he joked or flirted.

"I'm kidding. Relax. If it's bugging you that much, then send her a text or call her asking if you pissed her off in some way. From what you've told me, she's blunt. I'm sure she won't beat around the bush if you did."

Abby was right. If there was one thing he had learned about Charlotte, it was she wasn't afraid to tell it like it was. She was a straight shooter and he preferred that.

"Maybe later." He shrugged. Knowing full well the moment he was done with lunch he would be taking her advice and texting Charlotte. He had it bad and just the thought that she might be avoiding him didn't sit well.

"When is the SWAT test?" Abby expertly changed the subject.

"Next month."

"You got your head in the game?" she asked with her eyebrows raised, popping a French fry in her mouth.

Taking a bite of his own burger, he chewed the bite before answering.

"It will be."

There wasn't much more to say than that. Two months ago it was all he could think about. Now his mind was preoccupied with a certain redhead who lived too far away. He had even gone as far as looking at departments in and around Boston, but he quickly stopped once he realized how pathetic that would look if he one day mentioned he had been looking. Especially since Charlotte never mentioned that she even wanted to try a relationship with him even if they were living in the same area.

They finished their meal in comfortable silence before heading their separate ways. Climbing back into his cruiser, he sent a message out to Charlotte before he lost his nerve.

Brooks: Did someone kidnap you or are you just hiding from me today lol ;)

He hoped Charlotte would take his bantering for what it was, a way to show that the conversation from the previous evening wasn't meant to freak her out. It wasn't like he planned to drop down on his knee that very same day or knock her up so she would be tied to him. Hell, he would be happy with a date at some point. It was only a few agonizing minutes later when his phone finally beeped. He pulled it out from the cup holder and read her response.

Charlotte: Sorry, I guess I only responded to your text this morning in my head. I thought it was strange you were being so quiet today.

Okay, so maybe the whole thing was just a misunderstanding. And to think he had spent all morning overanalyzing everything he had said to her. He wasn't sure when he became such an insecure fool, but he wasn't fond of it. Charlotte was doing crazy things to his heart and head.

Brooks: Oh good, you are alive. I was getting ready to send in the National Guard. Phew, that would have been embarrassing.

He added a silly face for good measure. He never used to use emojis in his texts. But Charlotte had him doing a lot of new things it would seem.

Charlotte: Yes, that would have been awkward. How is your shift going?

Brooks: Good. Just had lunch with Abby. She said to say hello

Charlotte had asked him about his job often enough that she pretty much knew who he worked with. He thought it best to be open about his friendship with Abby since it was really the only other woman he spoke to.

Charlotte: Tell her I said hi back and I can't wait to meet her. We can swap stories

He froze when he read the message. Did that mean she planned to visit? That she wanted to meet his friends? She never mentioned it before, and he wasn't sure if it was even intentional now.

Brooks: She would love that

There was nothing else to say. He didn't want to freak her out by asking the million and one questions that were running through his mind. After last night, the last thing he wanted was to possibly scare her off again. He was at home plate in the last inning with two outs and he had just swung his first strike. Two more and the game was over.

Charlotte: Trista is coming to town tonight. She's stopping in for an appointment and then we are going out

He racked his brain trying to remember who Trista was. He knew there was some chick who she worked with. A young girl who was interning to be a fashion designer but that didn't make sense. The person was supposed to be stopping in for an appointment. Plus, she told him about the disaster nightclub they went to the night before he showed up. Then it clicked.

Brooks: That's the model, right? The one who is friends with one of the Charlie Team women.

He remembered Leslie giving him a rundown at the wedding, but he had been too distracted at the time. He didn't recognize the name as any of the wives or girlfriends, so it must be one of the friends he concluded.

Charlotte: Yes! Trista St. Clair. I had almost died when I found out Ash knew her and would introduce us. She's my ultimate girl crush.

He pulled up a picture of Trista on his phone. Almost every one of them was her on the runway or at some event. She was certainly stunning, but he much preferred the natural beauty he found in Charlotte.

Brooks: Girl crush huh? I mean I'm all for it as long as I can watch lol ;)

He hit send before his mind fully registered what he had said. He was about to apologize when her response came through.

Charlotte: If Trista wanted to hook up with me, I would totally let you watch.

Swerving his patrol car, he nearly caused an accident when he read her text. Putting his phone away, he chastised himself for texting and driving. He had sent his message while at a stoplight and it had turned green right before she messaged back. He had been so caught up wanting to see what she said that he had broken his golden rule. Pulling into a parking lot, he reread the message before sending his reply.

Brooks: Deal

He was a possessive man, so the thought of sharing wasn't really an option, but the fact that she had continued the banter made him smile. Gone were any lingering worries that he needed to watch what he sent her.

Charlotte: I better get ready for work. Trista and I will be getting drinks later, so sorry in advance if I go off the grid. I will be completely fangirling the whole time lol

Brooks: Ok lol. Have fun and be safe. Just let me know when you get home

Charlotte: Always (with a blushing face)

Not only wasn't she blowing him off, but she was acting just as she normally would. Feeling like things were okay and he had nothing to worry about, he put his phone away and focused on work.

Chapter 11

F angirling was an understatement. She had spent a solid hour in front of the mirror changing her outfit over and over again. Seven outfits later, she settled on a pair of high-waisted shorts with a tight tucked-in top and a pair of heels. It was simple yet fashionable. One of the few requirements her boss had for her. She could care less what she did, just as long as she looked good and made the clients happy. Wearing the most popular trend was a given as that was basically her job. She could show up in sweatpants if that were the hottest trend at the moment. Maybe she could make that happen. That way she could be comfortable all the time. Or maybe pajamas. The idea certainly appealed to her. Too bad she knew damn well her boss would never go for it. Oh well, a girl could hope.

Now Charlotte stood in the shop, admiring the dress that her boss made for Trista. It was designed to be worn to a gala in France next week. She was just a tad envious. Not about the dress, even though it was absolutely stunning, and Trista would look amazing in it, and not about the gala. There were going to be too many famous people and she would probably drool and make a complete ass of herself. No, she was envious that the gala was in France. It was the one place she wanted to visit so damn badly she would have sold her soul.

The door opening jarred her from her thoughts. Looking over her shoulder, a huge grin broke out on her face when Trista walked through the door.

"Hey, girly, it's so good to see your face again." She met Trista halfway and pulled her in for a hug.

"Oh, I know what you mean. The wedding wasn't even a month ago, but it feels so much longer."

Sporting a flowy dress and sandals, Trista only stood a couple of inches taller today. Unlike the first time they met, when Charlotte had mistakenly worn flip-flops. Trista was a solid eight inches taller. Yes, she asked, and it was clear as day when they stood next to each other that first time.

"Have you been busy?"

"Oh my God, yes," Trista groaned. "Between modeling shoots, galas, and trying to expand the organization with Wes, I haven't stopped traveling. I'm actually looking forward to spending some quality time in Texas soon. I'm going to take a few months off from shows to focus on getting everything set up."

Everyone was going to Texas it would seem. Leslie had mentioned the first time she introduced Trista that she was in the process of setting up an organization to help transition girls rescued from human trafficking back into the world. She didn't know all the details, but it sounded great, and from the way Trista was talking, things were going well.

"Speaking of galas, I have your dress!" She spun on her heels and dragged Trista toward the dress she was admiring before her friend showed up.

Dress wasn't the proper word. It was a silver gown with one thick strap that would go over her left shoulder and flow down her back. There was a slit on the opposite side clear up to her hip and a wide-open back. The strap would need to be taped down the day of as it was meant to just flow freely.

"Oh my! Lola outdid herself with this one. I can't wait to see what it looks like on!"

Lola was her boss. Trista was one of the few who called her by her name. Most just referred to her as "the bitch" since, more often than not, their exchanges were unpleasant. Moving towards the dressing area, Charlotte grabbed the shoes she'd previously picked out; they would match the dress perfectly.

"The silver is going to make your eyes pop! I went through dozens of fabrics until I found the one I envisioned," she told Trista, who was now behind the curtain changing.

Peeking her head out, Trista responded, "I'm not sure what Lola would do without you. Your style is always on point. I've seen your designs. Don't think the whole fashion world doesn't know who the true artist is."

Charlotte felt the heat rise in her cheeks at the compliment. At one time in her life, she thought about becoming a fashion designer, but while she had an eye for fashion and could describe what she thought would look best, she lacked the skill to draw it well. Not to mention she couldn't sew for shit. She needed someone else to take her ideas and turn them into a work of art. Which was exactly what her boss did. Fortunately, her boss recognized what she had in Charlotte and compensated her well for it.

It was several moments later before Trista threw open the curtain and stepped out with a slight spin. The strap flowing behind her like a veil.

"I'll make sure your team knows the shoulder needs to adhere to you when they come to pick it up," she said as Trista checked out the gown in the mirror.

"It's amazing," Trista said in awe. "I love it. And you're right, it brings out the silver in my eyes."

The gown was even more amazing on Trista. When she had originally suggested the design, Lola had questioned the sheer layer she wanted to be used specifically for the strap so it flowed like a train down the back. But seeing it on and the way it flowed each time Trista moved, she knew she had made the right choice.

"I'm so glad you love it." Tiny tears burned her eyes. It was pathetic, she knew but she couldn't begin to explain how happy it made her to know that Trista loved a dress that she dreamed up. When Trista had first appeared on the runway, Charlotte could remember telling Lola that she hoped one day she would appear in the shop looking for clothes. Little did she know at the time, it would only be months later when her own best friend had a connection, and she would get the chance to not only meet but become good friends with that same model.

"You have a talent and I know we have discussed this before, but you really need to consider designing on your own. If drawing isn't your thing, then hire people to make the designs you want. *You* are the brains here, it should be your name showcased," Trista insisted.

This wasn't a new discussion. Leslie had been the first one to plant the idea and she had considered it, but truthfully, she was scared. She was a no-name person trying to break out into a highly competitive world. She wasn't sure she had it in herself.

"We can discuss it more over drinks," Charlotte conceded. "I'm starved and you, my dear, were my last appointment for the day, so let's get out of here," she added with flair. She was ready to kick back and relax.

"Not that I want to invite myself over but that's exactly what I'm going to do. So what are your thoughts on stopping at the liquor store and ordering in? I want uninterrupted girl time that doesn't involve people wanting to take pictures with me or me hiding."

Trista looked sheepish. Doing a mental walk-through of her apartment to make sure she cleaned up before leaving earlier, she answered, "Sure, why not? I much prefer comfy clothes anyway when I drink."

"Yes! Me too." Trista threw her hands up dramatically to emphasize her point. "Why sweatpants can't be the latest trend is beyond me. I mean, come on! Everyone knows that's what they prefer to wear anyway, so why not just embrace it?"

They both laughed, knowing it was the truth.

"Okay, let me get out of this and then we can get going."

While Trista went back behind the curtain, she pulled out her phone and opened up the food app she used to order.

"What's your preference for food?" she yelled out. The dressing area wasn't large, but the curtains were thick, and if she spoke at a normal tone, the person getting changed never heard her. It was yet another reason there was never more than one client in the place at a time.

"I'm craving Chinese but will eat just about anything right now," Trista hollered back.

"Chinese it is."

She spent the next few minutes hashing out their dinner order while Trista finished changing. With the gown hung up and a note to contact Trista's team in the morning, she locked up and hailed a taxi. There was a small market just down the street from her apartment that had a great selection of wine, so after one quick stop, they were lounging in her living room with Chinese spread across the coffee table and wineglasses full.

"Oh, crap," she grumbled as she hopped up off the couch and ran to the kitchen for her phone.

"What's wrong?" Trista asked with concern.

"I forgot to text Brooks when I got in," she replied automatically while typing out a quick text.

Charlotte: Hey! Trista and I decided to eat and have drinks at my place tonight, so I'm home early

"Brooks as in Zack's brother?" Trista inquired. "That Brooks?"

She hadn't heard Trista enter the kitchen, so she jumped when her friend's voice was right behind her, casually looking over her shoulder with a chuckle.

Pulling the phone to her chest, she mumbled back, "Yes, that Brooks."

"Did you really store his number in your phone as Big Dick BFF?" The chuckle had turned into full-on laughter, big fat tears and all.

"Yes, I did," she huffed.

"Okay, I get the whole 'big dick' reference since I can imagine it probably is, but why BFF?"

"Um...because after we had amazing angry sex, I might have told him I only wanted to be friends," she replied sheepishly, no longer able to look her friend in the eye.

"Hold up," Trista started, palm up. "You're telling me you had amazing angry sex with a man who looks like a bronzed Olympian fucking god, and *then* proceeded to tell him you only wanted to be friends? And he *actually* still talks to you enough that you ran in here to tell him you're home?" The look on Trista's face could only be described as "What The Actual Fuck." If there was a book with common phrases and pictures of what people saying them looked like, Trista's face right that moment would be pictured next to that phrase.

"Yes." She winced.

"Are you fucking batshit crazy?!" Trista screamed with her hands thrown in the air.

"Probably," she admitted honestly.

"That man must be head over heels in love with you if he's willing to continue talking to you on the regular after you friend-zoned him. And don't think I didn't see that little blushy face from earlier. I bet you two are hardcore flirting. That, or some pretty damn good sexting."

The blush Trista so generously pointed out was now crawling its way up her neck in real time. Damn her pale skin. She couldn't hide that shit even if she wanted to. And since she rarely blushed, she had a feeling it was because Trista mentioned love. Sex never made her blush.

"No, we're not sexting," she said, rolling her eyes. "Geesh, why does everyone assume that? Am I that much of a slut?"

Trista opened her mouth to respond, but Charlotte put her hand up and interrupted, "No, don't answer that. And he's *not* in love with me. He's just being a nice guy. He will most likely forget I exist in a month, or sooner if he finds himself a girlfriend."

She tried not to show how much that thought hurt. It was silly. She was the one to recommend the whole friends only, so she had no right to get upset if and when he did get a girlfriend.

"I call bullshit."

Before Charlotte could respond, the phone beeped in her hand. Quickly pulling it from her chest, she looked to see what he had to say.

Big Dick BFF: Ok, have fun, and if I don't get to talk to you later, sweet dreams, beautiful

Charlotte: Night, hot stuff

"Aww, you even have cute little nicknames!" Trista didn't even try to hide that she was reading the messages. Slapping Charlotte's arm, she continued, "And you say it's just friendship. Phish. I'll say it again. BULLSHIT!" her friend shouted over her shoulder as she walked back to the living room.

Looking back down at her phone, she contemplated. Was he in love with her? She doubted it. He never said anything, and he easily agreed to the friendship. Not to mention he never once mentioned her going down there or him coming to her. Besides the one visit after she did her famous disappearing act, there were no other signs he was interested in anything serious.

Putting her phone back on the island, she went to join her friend. She had plans for the evening and they didn't include thinking about Mr. Hot Stuff. Those plans included lo mein and getting drunk on wine. All thoughts of relationships would have to wait until another time.

Chapter 12

One Month Later

The sound of her phone dinging nonstop pulled her from an amazing dream. She had been visiting Leslie in Texas when Brooks had shown up and demanded she go to his apartment with him. He had been growling something in her ear about how he controlled her orgasms when she was ripped out of that dream and forced to face the reality that she was in bed. Alone.

Ready to yell at whoever had the nerve to disrupt her wet dream, she saw the long line of messages on her locked screen. At some point, while she was sleeping, a group chat was started with her, Brooks, Leslie, and Zack. Groaning, she unlocked the screen and started to catch up on what she missed.

BFF's Annoying Husband: Psst...

BFF's Annoying Husband: Hey

BFF's Annoying Husband: Hey, Charlotte

BFF's Annoying Husband: Charlotte, are you ignoring me? It's rude to ignore your best friend's husband.

Badass Author Bitch: I told you she's probably still sleeping and likely to murder you

BFF's Annoying Husband: No way, she loves me

Badass Author Bitch: Not that much she doesn't

BFF's Annoying Husband: Ok, but she loves you and killing me would upset you so... I'm safe lol

Big Dick BFF: Why am I included in this torture? Other than to witness a crime in which I will be forced to lie that I knew nothing about

BFF's Annoying Husband: Because Charlotte also loves you, so she won't murder you either

Big Dick BFF: You seem pretty confident she won't murder you but I'm willing to bet the odds aren't in your favor

Badass Author Bitch: And we all know how much you love to bet, dear

Big Dick BFF: And lose. Don't forget he always loses

BFF's Annoying Husband: Har har. You think you guys are so funny

Badass Author Bitch: Pretty much

Big Dick BFF: Kinda

BFF's Annoying Husband: Oh, Charlotte...

BFF's Annoying Husband: Where are you?

BFF's Annoying Husband: Come save me from these two meanies.

She didn't want to save him but she certainly considered murdering the man. She didn't give a shit if he was married to her best friend. She was young enough. She could find love again or at least a man to pleasure her for the rest of her days.

Charlotte: Why the fuck would I save your ass when it just woke me up?

BFF's Annoying Husband: Charlotte, you're alive. I'm so glad to hear it. I was getting concerned.

She rolled her eyes at Zack's dramatics. How Leslie dealt with him was beyond her. Especially first thing in the morning.

Badass Author Bitch: I told you she would be sleeping

Big Dick BFF: For the record, so was I. Worked an overnight and just nodded off when your stupid ass started this nonsense.

BFF's Annoying Husband: Charlotte, do you see how mean they are to me. I simply wanted to see how you were doing this fine morning.

Charlotte: You brought this on yourself, and just so you know, I would murder you and wouldn't feel an ounce of remorse. Leslie is young and hot, she could easily find herself a new man.

Big Dick BFF: Hahahaha burn

Badass Author Bitch: LOL she's right, you know

BFF's Annoying Husband: You guys are mean. I don't know why I talk to you

Charlotte: You're the one who started this crap and for what?

BFF's Annoying Husband: Because I have a secret and Leslie said I couldn't tell anyone until she talked to you

Big Dick BFF: So you included me why?

BFF's Annoying Husband: Because, asshole, you were the first person I wanted to tell. Keep your shit up and you will be the last.

Charlotte: What secret?

Okay, she had to admit now she was wide awake and wanted to know what the secret was. It was a weakness of hers.

Badass Author Bitch: SURPRISE!!! Auntie Charlotte

The picture of a positive pregnancy test flashed on her screen. Throwing the covers off, she squealed. Hitting the dial button, it took Leslie only one ring to answer.

"Oh my God, oh my God, oh my God! Is this for real? You're pregnant?! I'm going to get to be an aunt!" she continued to squeal. The pitch in her voice rising with each sentence.

"Yup," Leslie confirmed. "Took the test this morning. Three actually," she laughed. "All of them said the same thing. Zack and I are going to be parents!"

"Yay. I'm so happy for you. Okay, so maybe I won't kill Zack after all. I mean the baby deserves to meet their father. Even if said father is a royal pain in the ass."

"He was prepared to text you hours ago. I had to distract him a bit." Leslie giggled like a schoolgirl.

"I can only imagine what that distraction consisted of."

"It was fun is all I'm going to say."

"I bet. Congratulations! I really am happy for you, and I can tell the two of you are excited."

Zack's laughter in the background couldn't be missed. As well as his occasional off-key singing. Happy wasn't the word. She was surprised he wasn't banging on his chest like a caveman since he knocked up his wife. Although since she wasn't there, there was no way to prove that didn't happen already.

"We are. I know the 'oh shit' part is coming soon though. We had talked about starting to try but I thought I would have more time. Zack's swimmers, on the other hand, had their own plans."

"And I'm betting he is bragging about that," she joked.

"You have no idea. Super swimmers are what he has been calling them all morning. The man is insane."

"Yes, but you love that insane man and married him. And will now have his baby."

"Yeah, I do and will." Her friend sighed wistfully. It was the only way to describe how dreamlike her best friend's voice turned at the mention of having Zack's baby.

"Well, you two go continue celebrating while I wake up some more. I'll talk to you more later and we will plan a visit. I want to see my best friend in person now that she's knocked up."

"Absolutely. Get your ass down here."

She clicked off, but before she could toss her phone on the bed, she noticed a few more messages. It appeared Zack and Brooks had continued to chat for a bit while she was talking to Leslie, but she also noticed another message from just Brooks.

Big Dick BFF: Good morning, beautiful. Sorry my obnoxious brother woke you up

Charlotte: Morning and it's ok. He's forgiven only because of the news. Otherwise, I probably would have offed him

Big Dick BFF: It was pretty amazing news. Although I still can't believe I get to be an uncle

Charlotte: I know, it's crazy, right

Charlotte: I told Leslie I need to make a trip down now that she found out, so we can celebrate

Big Dick BFF: So that means you're coming to Texas. Any chance I get to see you as well?

Her stomach did the little flipping thing as she read the text. Was it supposed to do that when friends hung out? It didn't with Leslie. At least not in the same exact way.

Charlotte: Of course. I can't come all that way and not see my other BFF

His response was the blushing emoji, and for some reason, that simple text set a new round of butterflies off in her belly.

Big Dick BFF: Well, now that the excitement is over, I'm going to crash. I'll talk to you later. Have a good day at work.

Charlotte: Sleep well. Don't dream of me too much ;)

Did she really just say that. Looking down at her phone to verify, she smacked her hand against her forehead. Yup, she really said that. UGH. One of these days her big mouth was going to get her in trouble. When his only response back was a wink, she knew she was screwed all over again.

How was she supposed to see him in person? She hadn't thought that discussion fully through before she blurted out that she would make sure they hung out. It was one thing to flirt over text messages but to actually see him in person. She was likely to jump his bones the moment their eyes met. And then what? Friends with benefits? Could she even do something like that? No! her heart screamed. Of course, the damn thing was already involved. No matter how hard she tried to keep it on a leash, it never listened. Not that she really expected it would have.

Now that she was fully awake and there was nothing else to distract her, she figured it was time she got herself ready for the day.

Chapter 13

Was it normal to be this nervous? Probably not. Last week when he had jokingly asked if he would see her when she visited, he hadn't thought it through. Hadn't realized he would be this nervous. He didn't get nervous when he hung out with Abby. Not that he hung out with her outside of work, but still. They were just friends. Same as him and Charlotte. But that was a lie. There was nothing the same when it came to Charlotte. She was the exception to every rule. The beautiful, funny, smart, and sexy exception to everything he ever thought he knew he wanted.

It had been almost two months since he saw her and not once did his need for her change or diminish. If anything, it only grew stronger. He looked forward to waking up and sending her a text, although he knew anything before ten in the morning might result in bodily harm. He couldn't wait to talk to her in the evenings when she got off work, and the days he couldn't talk were physically hard. He had become dependent on her.

Which brought him to his other dilemma. What if he saw her in person and screwed all that up? Things were going so well that the last thing he wanted was to do something stupid like try to kiss her the moment he laid eyes on her. So instead of having her come back to his place like he originally planned, he was now meeting her at his brother's place where she was planning to stay while on her visit. That way they had supervision and there wasn't a chance of angry sex against the kitchen counter.

Something he needed to stop thinking about unless he wanted to pull into his brother's driveway with his dick as hard as a fucking rock. Zack was likely to harass him, and he doubted Leslie would let it slide either. Charlotte, on the other hand, would probably say something crude that would only make him that much harder. He was fucked. There were no two ways about it. Absolutely, one hundred percent, fucked.

And now he was out of time. He pulled into his brother's driveway and parked his truck behind his brother's Jeep. Turning off the ignition, he leaned his head back on the seat and closed his eyes for a moment, willing his dick to listen. A rap on the window startled him. Pulling open the door, Zack chuckled.

"Trying to get rid of a major boner?" Zack wiggled his eyebrows.

He called it. Damn, he knew his brother well and vice versa.

"Fuck off, asshole."

There was nothing else to say. They both knew it was the truth. He and Zack had talked multiple times about Charlotte. As much as he called his younger brother an asshole often enough, they were actually pretty close. And even more so now that Leslie was back in his life. He found himself talking to his brother and wife several times a week. It was usually Leslie who reached out first but that didn't change the fact that their relationship was closer now than it ever was before.

He climbed out, finished rearranging himself since his dick apparently had a mind of its own today, and ignored Zack's laughter. His brother could kiss his ass as far as he was concerned.

When they got into the house, he was greeted with a hug from his sister-in-law. He wasn't sure what he expected since obviously at only a couple of weeks she wouldn't be showing, but the way she glowed was impressive. She had always been a naturally beautiful person, but at that moment, she was radiant. It was like nothing but happiness oozed from her pores.

"You look amazing," he whispered in her ear. "I hope my brother is taking care of you."

"He's spoiling me rotten," she laughed in return. "Even more so since we found out. He claims it's his way of spoiling the baby."

"Already? That's going to be one spoiled child by the time it's born. The first grandchild and niece or nephew," he chuckled.

"Oh, your parents already admitted they fully plan on spoiling him or her. They want to know the minute we find out the gender."

"I vote girl." Charlotte raised her hand as she joined them in the entryway.

All he could do was stare. While Leslie was glowing from pregnancy, Charlotte was just beautiful in every way. She took his breath away. It might be cliche, but it was the truth nonetheless. How could a woman be more beautiful every time he saw her?

Say something, dickhead, before she thinks there is something wrong with you.

"Hey." He stepped in for an awkward hug.

Smooth, dumbass, real smooth.

"Hey yourself," Charlotte replied with a smile.

Why did her smile have to light up the whole room or instantly turn him into a bubbling fool? Not to mention the damn somersault his stomach just did. When was the last time he was this nervous around someone? Middle school?

"Yeah, well, you only want a girl so you can use her like a dress-up doll," Leslie cut in with a knowing smile. Thank God for that save.

"Use is such a harsh word. I like to think of it as having the most fashionable niece around and we both know that without me, you would be lost."

"True. Okay, I'll give you that."

"Doesn't matter. It's going to be a boy," Zack stated. His chest puffed out like a proud papa bear.

"Would you like to bet on it?" Brooks asked jokingly.

"Nah, I'm already pretty sure about it, so I refuse to jinx it with a bet. But I'm pretty sure once I tell the team, you know they'll be all over placing bets. You can join them."

He might just do that. He didn't care either way but what kind of brother would he be if he didn't bet against what Zack wanted. Certainly not the kind he was used to.

"You boys are relentless. You will bet on anything," Leslie huffed.

"The guys bet on Arlo's kid, so it's a safe assumption they will do the same this time. I can't wait to tell them." His brother was overexcited as he rubbed his hands together, a huge smile on his face.

"I'm surprised you kept your mouth shut this long," Charlotte threw out.

"Only because she made me." Zack threw a thumb in the direction of Leslie. "She said we had to wait until at least the first ultrasound."

Was that a whine in his brother's voice? It sure sounded like it. He was a sniper, for fuck's sake, but he had zero patience in his personal life. Maybe Kade did all the work? That made more sense.

"I could make you wait until we get through the first trimester at fourteen weeks." Leslie placed her hands on her hips, squaring up with her husband.

"I love you, LeLe." Zack grabbed his wife's hips and pulled her in. "More than anything else in the world."

The whining voice was gone and replaced with groveling. Brooks was tempted to laugh but figured if his brother didn't kill him, his sister-in-law might. He had heard pregnant women's emotions were like a roller coaster. He wasn't brave enough to test that theory. So instead, he moved closer to Charlotte to give the two lovebirds a private moment.

Standing shoulder to shoulder, he leaned down to whisper, "I'm happy to see your face. I missed that smile."

A blush crept up her neck and cheeks. That was new.

"Same." She smiled.

He wasn't used to her being shy. Every other time they had been in the same room or even talked on the phone, she was loud and usually the center of attention. This was different and he wasn't entirely sure how he felt about it.

"So what are the plans for this evening?" he asked casually.

He shoulder-bumped her, a chuckle escaping her lips. There was the sweet sound he preferred. Now if he could just get the sassy mouth to join it, all would be right in the world.

"A movie and popcorn."

"My favorite." He winked.

"Correction, a chick flick. One sappy enough to make you cry," she challenged.

Turning so that he was facing her, he leaned in close. "I guess I'll bring the tissues and the shoulder to cry on."

"Smartass." She poked his chest, but the smile still remained.

"Sassy," he threw back at her.

"Ahem! Are you two done flirting over there?" Leslie casually asked.

Slowly turning his head, he glared at his no-longer-favorite sister-in-law. So much for her having his back. She smiled innocently in return. He wasn't buying it at all.

"We were just discussing the movie options for tonight," he ground out.

"Oh good. What decision did you make?"

"A chick flick. A real tearjerker," Charlotte told Leslie.

Zack groaned while Leslie chuckled. A silent communication passing between the two women. One he wished he understood but was terrified of at the same time.

"Bring it on, beautiful," Brooks goaded. "The men can handle it."

Famous last words.

Chapter 14

Why in the world did she think this would be a good idea? Nothing good could come of watching a movie on the same couch with Brooks. Especially since she'd been curled up on her own side, minding her own damn business, when he had pulled her feet so they were lying across his lap. And to make it worse, okay, really better, he was giving her a foot massage; a goddamn, amazingly relaxing, almost orgasmic fucking foot massage. She was in hell. A glorious fucking hell but still hell nonetheless, and apparently, at some point over the last ten minutes, she had become a whining bitch that even she was likely to slap. Talk about a mental breakdown.

"You're going to get wrinkles if you keep frowning like that," Leslie whispered from her spot on the couch.

Zack and Leslie had purchased a fixer-upper and it wasn't until recently that they had finally finished all the projects they had going. The living room was absolutely stunning. With a large open floor plan, they had placed a long L-shaped couch to separate the living room and dining room. All four of them were currently sprawled out on the couch with her and Leslie in the corner with their legs spread in opposite directions toward the men.

"How do you know I'm frowning? You're too busy watching the damn movie," she whispered back.

"Because I know you. I felt you tense when Brooks first pulled on your feet, and you keep going back and forth between relaxed and tense. Just relax and enjoy the time," Leslie chided.

Damn her observant friend. She hadn't realized how much her body had given away while she was having her internal debate. She took a chance and looked over at Brooks. He was still watching the movie, so she was able to observe the way his arms flexed as his thumbs pushed into the pads of her foot. The man sure knew how to give a foot massage. As if he could sense her watching him, he looked her way. Giving her a lopsided smile and wink before returning his gaze to the movie.

Damn, the man had a nice smile. He'd probably won his fair share of hearts and, when he smiled, hot damn it was panty dropping. She should know, she's dropped hers twice already. Okay, more like once-ish. The second time she hadn't been wearing any. And just like that, she was wet. The complete opposite of what she wanted for the evening. Turning her head back to the movie, she tried thinking of anything that would kill the lust.

Saying the alphabet backward. Nope. And way harder than one would think. Counting to one hundred. Also nope. Thinking back to her smelly high school science teacher who gave her the creeps. Nope. Actually, that one helped a bit. She would need to remember that for future reference.

"Tell me again why we let the women pick the movie tonight?" Zack grumbled.

"Because happy wife, happy life, and since this wife is currently carrying your child and nauseous nonstop, it was better to just agree," Leslie replied sweetly.

"Right. Love you and you're doing such an amazing job." Zack smiled from ear to ear.

Charlotte was torn between wanting to gag at the sickly sweetness or laugh hysterically at how easily the big bad sniper, whose job was to literally kill people, could be so easily intimidated by his tiny-ass, pregnant wife.

"You're such a kiss ass," Brooks laughed.

Zack threw a handful of popcorn at his brother. Grumbling again, "Just you wait, dickhead."

What did Zack mean by that? Wait for Brooks to fall in love, or get someone knocked up? And why did the thought of either of those possibilities make her want to throw something?

"Relax." Leslie nudged her with a chuckle and a shake of the head.

Damn, she was becoming way too transparent. Time to add poker dealer to that "if I ever lose my job and need to find a new career" not-happening list. The damn list was going to be a mile long at the rate she was going.

"I am relaxed," she hissed back.

"No, you're tense because Zack practically mentioned another woman in your presence when in reality, he meant you."

This time, she whipped her head first towards Leslie and then Brooks, who was looking back at her with his eyebrows raised and his head tilted slightly. Waving him off she glared back at Leslie before returning to the movie.

Despite being the one to choose the movie, she held zero interest in watching Shane West and Mandy Moore out on the dock in the dark, as he admits that he might kiss her and her breathless reply of "I might be bad at it." She had watched the movie a million times, so she knew every word and every scene. She didn't need to be looking at the screen to know they had just shared their first chaste kiss.

No, she had other things she would rather be doing, like side-glancing at Brooks. Man, the way he let his stubble grow out when he wasn't working. She used to prefer a clean face; there was something to be said about a strong jaw and chin, but now she found she rather appreciated a little facial hair. Especially when that hair was on the face of the man whose hands were still doing wonders to her feet.

They continued to watch the movie in comfortable silence. As the evening wore on, she felt herself nodding off. She wasn't sure if it was the movie or the foot rub or a combination of both but her eyes began to feel heavy. Scooching herself a bit lower until her head was resting against the cushion, she got comfortable.

It was dark when she woke up to a blanket tucked up to her chin and a strong pair of arms wrapped around her middle. She didn't need to look to know who those arms belonged to, but she turned her head anyway. As expected, Brooks was spooning her from behind, his body on the outside of her blanket. Listening to his even breaths, she slowly drifted back to sleep.

When she woke up again, to pans banging in the kitchen, Brooks's arms were no longer holding her. She had almost convinced herself it was just a dream until he sauntered over with a coffee mug in his hand. Placing it on the table in front of her, he sat on the same table, hands on his knees in front of her.

"Morning, beautiful. You know, it's kind of nice to say that in person rather than just a text message," he chuckled.

Taking a long sip to both wake her up and give her mind time to formulate a proper response, she responded, "Morning and yes, right back at ya."

"Did you sleep well?"

"Like a baby, but I could have sworn I woke up in the middle of the night wrapped in some sexy man's arms, but I must have been dreaming because they were gone this morning." She shrugged. Falling back to their usual bantering.

His only response was a wide, sexy grin. She wondered what he was thinking but didn't get the chance to ponder it any further when Zack plopped down on the other end of the couch.

"Oh look, sleeping beauty has finally decided to grace us with her presence."

"It's barely morning. I'm normally still sleeping at this hour."

"So I've heard. Repeatedly. From my fabulous wife every time I attempt to call or text you." Zack grinned.

"And yet you still make the mistake of waking me up earlier than I like." She raised her eyebrow as she took a sip of coffee, letting the caffeine hit do what it was meant to do.

"I figured since you haven't sent a hitman yet, I'm pretty safe." He shrugged back casually.

"He's on order. I assure you."

Both Leslie and Brooks snickered at her remark. Zack started to but stopped when he noticed her face was still neutral.

"You are joking, right?" he asked.

Her only response was to shrug her shoulder while continuing to savor her morning coffee. Let him figure out if she were serious or not. Maybe it would keep him from annoying her first thing in the morning for a while. Probably not, but it was worth a shot.

"Now that we've established there may or may not be a hit out on my husband, can we discuss plans for the day? I know it's still early, but I want to do some baby shopping or at least window shopping while my best friend is here."

"I second that plan." Charlotte raised her hand.

They spent the next thirty minutes deciding where they wanted to go and bickering about hitmen. Apparently, Zack woke up in a whining mood that morning and wouldn't let it go until she finally admitted she hadn't, in fact, hired anyone. And then he proceeded to argue some more that he didn't believe her. By the time they finally left they house, she was pretty sure even Leslie was contemplating the hitman idea. And as her best friend, she would fully support and help with the plan if needed. What else were friends for?

Chapter 15

There were times that working overnights sucked. This was one of those times. Not that he ever had plans. In fact, since Zack's wedding, he had barely done more than grab a drink when one of his brothers showed up or when one of the guys from work asked. He wasn't complaining. He had no interest in going out. He liked his nights at home where he spoke to Charlotte, laughing at whatever nonsense she came up with in the moment. Most days he rushed home just to have that time with her. Was it pathetic? Probably, but at the moment he didn't care. He was just glad to have the little connection he could to her.

A month had gone by since his visit to his brother's house. A whole month since he had the pleasure of seeing Charlotte and falling asleep with her in his arms, even if it wasn't intentional. When she had passed out, he had taken the opportunity to snuggle up. He could have easily gone to the guest bedroom, but at the time, he threw caution to the wind and decided to take the rare opportunity. When she woke up and joked with him about it, he knew he made the right decision. He was going to steal any moments he could. He didn't get the chance again.

She returned to Boston a few days later and they were back to status quo. They texted often and spoke almost daily, but not once was anything other than friendship discussed. As far as he could tell, she wasn't dating anyone, and he certainly wasn't. He was too busy prepping for the SWAT test or working. That was the case tonight.

Maybe another visit was in order. Maybe he could convince her to let him come up to Boston on his next days off. Friends visited each other, right? She visited Leslie, so he could play it off like that. He was solidifying his plans when reports of a third party calling about possible screaming in an alley came across his radio. He was only two blocks away, so he called en route.

He turned his cruiser into the dark alley and came to a rolling stop. All of the businesses were closed, and he didn't hear anything out of the ordinary. Radioing that he was on the scene, he stepped out of his patrol car and flicked on his flashlight. There was a dumpster about ten feet away that smelled like it hadn't been picked up in a while. The protruding bags only confirmed his thoughts.

His backup was still a couple of blocks away, so he slowly moved through the alley with his gun drawn and flashlight sweeping the corners.

The alley was just over a block long, with the backs of businesses on both sides. Some of those businesses had lights above the back doors but most were burnt out. Apartments lined the top of the buildings with fire escapes along the way. The alley was eerily quiet for just after midnight. He expected to hear noise from some of the apartments or from shops closing up.

He was about to radio in that the call was unfounded when a bump next to the dumpster caught his attention. Pivoting himself that way, he shone his flashlight on what he assumed was a young man. His first thought was homeless, but the clothes were too clean. The hood of a sweatshirt hid the man's face, or at least what he assumed was a man, based on the clothing and size.

"Did you call nine-one-one for someone screaming?" he asked.

The hair on the back of his neck was now standing up and he had an uneasy feeling. He wished his backup would show already.

The person didn't answer but continued to move his way. Planting his feet, he raised his gun just in case. The man had his hands in his pockets and was giving off bad vibes.

"I'm going to need you to stop and raise your hands in the air slowly," he sternly advised.

The man stopped in his tracks. Without raising his head, he took one hand out but not the other. Brooks's uneasiness was intensifying by the second. He could hear sirens coming closer, so he knew his backup was on the way.

"Show me your other hand!" he yelled over the sound of the sirens. They were slightly deafening in the silent alley.

"It's your fault she's dead, Officer Brooks Lynch," the man mumbled while whipping his hand out of his pocket.

It took a split second for Brooks to register that the man held a gun and was firing his way. The delay was deadly as he felt the first shot enter his shoulder. It knocked him backward, but he managed to fired his own gun, just as another shot hit him, this time in the vest. With a burning chest and throbbing shoulder, he again fired off a few shots, but his vision began to blur as he took a third shot in the vest. Falling backward, his head smacked against the street with a thud.

The sound of feet hitting pavement pounded in his ears.

"George 804, we have an officer down. I repeat, officer down!" he heard as someone leaned down to check his pulse.

His chest hurt like a bitch, and he could feel the blood pooling around his shoulder. His head continued to spin, and he wanted to throw up, but tried his damndest to swallow it down. He began to see black dots cloud his vision and knew he was just moments away from passing out. The voices of his comrades sounded like they were deep down in a tunnel.

And all he could think about was Charlotte. Her smiling face. Her sass. The way she called him out and didn't take his crap. How her voice sounded every time she called him "hot stuff" and how nicely her body fit against his. He should have been more honest with her, should have told her how he felt rather than hiding away. Now he wasn't sure he would get the chance.

He didn't think he had life-threatening wounds, but his body had gone numb and he barely understood when someone mentioned that an ambulance was on the way. He was too tired to stay awake. If he could just rest a minute, then he would be okay. Closing his eyes, he had one final thought before darkness took hold.

What the fuck did that guy mean it was my fault she was dead?

Chapter 16

"Are you sure you don't want to go out tonight?" Michelle asked for the fifth time. "A few of my friends are just grabbing drinks at the bar near my house. They wouldn't mind having one more join."

Charlotte hadn't gone out with her co-worker since the last disastrous visit to the club. Not because Michelle hadn't invited her. In fact, she did so often. It was odd, considering that, apart from the long-ass hour wait to get into the club, they didn't hang out together at all that night. So why would Charlotte want a repeat? Most of the time, she had some excuse she could use, but tonight was the first time she was blatantly lying.

"Sorry, I have plans tonight but maybe next time," she responded as she locked up, hailing a cab before Michelle could ask what those plans were.

Those plans usually included either talking to Leslie or Brooks, but both were busy. Leslie was having a date night with her hubby, and while the thought of getting all the dirty details used to appeal to her, that was no longer the case. There was something weird about hearing about her man's brother doing the dirty.

My man? Since when did I start thinking of him as mine?

It might have something to do with the fact that, despite the physical part of it or lack of, they might as well be in a relationship. She hadn't even so much as looked at another man since having sex with Brooks, and he certainly hadn't mentioned another woman. They spoke almost every night when he wasn't working, and they were texting all the time. And then there was the flirting. They couldn't make it through a single conversation without some type of flirting. And yet with all of that happening, she still insisted it was a friends-only relationship.

Denial much?

So, since Brooks was working the night shift and Leslie was bumping uglies, she was left with only one option: finding a new book boyfriend to get lost in. She was due for a new one, or two. All of her usual authors didn't have books coming out currently, and Leslie was still writing and said it would be at least another few weeks before she could beta. Her tbr list was a mile long, so there were lots of options. It was just a matter of picking one.

As she walked into her apartment, she kicked off her shoes and started pulling her dress over her head before she even made it out of the living room. Living alone had its perks. She could walk around naked, and no one cared; even if she had a roommate, she wouldn't care.

I mean, if they can't accept me for who I am, then they don't deserve to be my roomie anyway.

Throwing on her usual pajama pants and a hoodie, she grabbed her tablet and began scrolling through her list. She found a rom-com that she thought fit her mood, and settled in for what was most likely going to be a long night. She wasn't a quitter, so she wouldn't put the book down until she either finished it or was so tired she passed out. Those were the only acceptable options in her mind.

The sound of her phone ringing startled her. Based on the tablet lying facedown on the comforter and the kink in her neck, it was safe to say she fell asleep while reading. She was trying to locate her phone in the dim light, cursing whoever kept calling. Every time she thought it was going to stop, it started all over again. Finally finding the damn thing buried in her sheets, she clicked accept without even looking to see who it was.

"What?" she hissed to whoever the unlucky recipient was.

"Oh my God, it's about damn time you answered!" Leslie cried out.

Pulling the phone away from her ear, she checked the caller ID just in case. While it sounded like her best friend, it didn't at the same time. Something was wrong.

"Leslie? What's wrong? Is everything okay? Why are you calling so late? Wait, what time is it anyway?"

She was firing off questions and not allowing Leslie time to answer any of them. She stopped and took a deep breath, hoping that whatever the reason was for the late-night call, it didn't have anything to do with the baby.

"It's Brooks," her friend whispered. "He's been shot."

The relief at hearing that nothing was wrong with the baby was short-lived. Did she just say Brooks had been shot?

"I'm sorry, what?"

Her brain was no longer working. She couldn't possibly have heard Leslie correctly. Brooks shot? A million thoughts and images slammed into her all at once. Putting a hand to her chest, she tried to take another breath, but it was like someone was sitting on her. No matter how hard she tried, she couldn't breathe.

"Charlotte? Are you still there? CHARLOTTE!"

Leslie's voice was echoing through the phone as Charlotte swung her legs over the edge of the bed, dropped her head between them and focused on her breathing. It had been years since she had a panic attack and she wasn't even sure if that's what this was, but she used the same techniques her doctor had taught her. When she finally felt like she could talk again, she pulled the phone back up to her ear.

"I'm here."

"You scared the shit out of me! Don't you know you shouldn't give a pregnant woman a heart attack like that!" Leslie chided her.

"I'm sorry, I didn't mean to. Did I hear you correctly? Brooks was shot? Is he okay? I mean I would hope so since you're not freaking out, but I need you to tell me the truth," she begged.

"No, I'm sorry, my emotions are all over the place, and when you stopped talking, I freaked," Leslie apologized. "Yes, he was shot at work tonight. He's in surgery now but expected to make a full recovery. Two of the shots hit his vest and the third hit him in the shoulder. I don't have any other details. Zack and I are on our way to Austin now. His parents called us and we are meeting them there."

Okay, so not life-threatening. That was good. Without knowing it, she started going over her schedule for the week, trying to remember which clients she had coming in and which ones she could easily pawn off to Michelle. Most were just coming in to try stuff on, which meant it wasn't a big deal if she was there or not, but she had one new client that she was meeting to get a feel for what she would like.

Biting on her nail, she weighed her options. She finally made up her mind and said, "I'm coming, too. I will catch the first flight out in the morning."

"Wait, what?"

"I'm flying down," Charlotte replied, with an implied *duh*. "I want to be there for him while he's recovering."

She had made up her mind and no one was going to change it. Michelle could easily handle the clients who were just picking up, and if it came down to it, she would video chat with the new client. The woman was a friend of Trista's; she would understand an emergency.

"Honey, are you sure that's a good idea?"

"Yes, I'm sure," she rushed out. "If it were you lying in that hospital, I would be there in a heartbeat. Brooks means just as much to me as you do. And I know in my heart that if the situation were reversed, he would be here for me."

"Okay, if that's what you want."

"It is," she insisted. "I'll text you once I have the flight information. Make sure to keep me updated." Without waiting for a response, she ended the call and tossed the phone on the nightstand.

Leslie said he was expected to make a full recovery but that didn't mean she didn't want to be kept in the loop. Nothing was guaranteed and, until she saw him for herself, she wasn't going to assume anything or believe anyone. Reaching for her tablet, she opened her browser and began searching for flights. The major perk of living in a city with an international airport meant there was usually no shortage of flights, especially when she would be flying into another major city.

With her flight booked, she hastily threw clothes into a bag, not really looking to see what she was grabbing. If she forgot anything, she could buy it there. Since it was still early and Lola was even less of a morning person than she was, she opted for a text message explaining that she had a family emergency out of town. There was a good chance that once her boss woke up, she would get an attitude about the last-minute notice, but she didn't give a shit. With another quick message to Michelle explaining that she would forward her client schedule and detailed explanations as soon as she checked into the airport, she looked around one last time to see if she missed anything. Confident she had what she needed, she quickly threw on a pair of yoga pants and a shirt. Grabbing her keys, phone, and carry-on, she was out the door within thirty minutes of Leslie calling.

She had been lucky enough to score one of the first flights out, but she still arrived way earlier than she needed to. Once she was through security and waiting in the terminal, she took the time to get herself in order. She looked like a mess but there was no time to correct it. Not that anyone would care, and she wasn't there to impress anyone. Well, except maybe Brooks's parents. Fortunately, they had met her before and knew her current ragged look wasn't a daily occurrence.

She passed the time drafting emails on her phone. She sent Michelle a very detailed report of the clients who would be coming in, pending communication to them; so detailed that even a toddler would be able to figure out the instructions. It was a good thing she was compulsively organized at work and never left until everything was ready. It sure saved her ass this time.

The next few emails were to the clients that she would be sending off to Michelle. She apologized profusely for having to go out of town but reassured each one that everything was still taken care of. She was known for not contacting a client until their order was complete. It saved her the headache of having to reschedule.

The last email was to her new client that she was supposed to interview. Not wanting to completely blow her off, she explained the situation and asked for a virtual conference instead, or to reschedule. She would leave it up to her to decide. With everything taken care of, she grabbed something to eat and waited for her flight to start boarding.

Chapter 17

"**I**s he going to be okay?"

He thought he heard talking around him, but his head felt like it was too stuffed full of cotton balls to understand what was going on.

How did I get here and why do I feel so tired?

A memory of him riding in the back of an ambulance flashed before his eyes. The medic telling him to stay awake. Just as quickly as the memory appeared it faded away. He could barely make out the other voice in the room before the pull of sleep dragged him back under.

The sound of Charlotte's laughter grabs his attention. She's sitting on a blanket with a little girl. Looking around, he realizes they are in his backyard except now there is a swing set and a little pink playhouse. They certainly weren't there before, and whose little girl was that? It couldn't be Zack and Leslie's. She had the same color hair as Charlotte. 'Daddy,' the little girl squealed as she jumped up and ran towards the side of the house. Looking that way, he was surprised to see himself, a few years older, lifting the giggling little girl into his arms and tickling her belly.

"Why hasn't he woken up yet?" This time he recognized the voice as his mother.

"It's only been a few hours since he came out of surgery. His body just needs time to heal."

He didn't care what his body needed. He wanted to get back to that dream he was just in. Did that mean he and Charlotte finally moved past "just friends"? And what about the little girl? She had called him daddy. Was that just wishful thinking or was he getting a glimpse into his future? He felt the familiar pull of sleep, but instead of fighting it, he gladly succumbed.

"Dad, can I borrow the car?" This time, he heard a young man. As with the last time, he was in his house except it was different. Bigger. As if he had expanded at some point. Moving through the entryway toward the voices, he entered the kitchen and found a much younger version of himself seated at the island while his older self and Charlotte stood on the other side. Whereas the young girl was a spitting image of Charlotte, there was no mistaking this young man as his son.

"Can you two stop that, it's gross?" The kid pretended to gag. He and Charlotte just giggled from their spot. Charlotte was in his arms, and he was nuzzling her neck. The moment brought a smile to his face. Even after however many years, they were still in love. At least from the little bit he saw so far.

"Can I please borrow the car before you two run away and have some adult time?" The word adult was emphasized with air quotes. Yup, this was definitely his son. He remembered giving his father similar grief any time he saw his parents making out.

"And where do you plan to go?" Charlotte twisted in his older self's arms until she was leaning back against his chest.

"Just out with some friends." The boy tried to shrug nonchalantly but he could tell he was hiding something.

The dream version of himself must have realized it as well because his eyes squinted, and in a serious voice he never thought he would ever hear coming out of his mouth, he said, "Don't you dare lie to your mother, son. We both raised you better than that. Now, the truth."

"Fine," his son started with a huff. "I want to take Laura to the movies," he finished, throwing himself back and crossing his arms.

The urge to laugh was real. Who knew teenage drama would be so funny? Before he could see how the rest of the conversation played out, he was back in the hospital bed.

"I hope you wake up soon. There is so much I want to tell you."

This time it was Charlotte's voice he heard. But that couldn't be right. She was in Boston, and he was home in Texas. He was in Texas, right? He couldn't remember anything before or after the ambulance ride. He had no idea why he was lying in a hospital bed. He tried to open his eyes, but they felt itchy, almost like sandpaper, and while he was screaming in his head that he wanted to hear what she had to say, there was no sound coming from his lips. He tried again to communicate but that familiar pull back to the dream state crept in. This time he tried to fight it, tried to stay with the present Charlotte, but sleep won out.

As with both times before, he recognized his house. Only this time several years had gone by. He could tell by the condition of some of the houses on his block. Sitting in a pair of rocking chairs on the porch, he recognized a very older version of himself and Charlotte. There was no talking. Just simply holding hands as the two of them rocked in unison. The sight brought tears to his eyes. They had grown old together.

As he woke this time, he was finally able to open his eyes and look around the room. Gone were the doctors and family members he had heard during his semi-conscience times. The only one left was his sleeping precious Charlotte. He no longer cared that she only wanted to be friends because he saw their future together, or what he hoped it would be. There was no way it was just a dream. It felt too real. All he needed to do was convince her it was meant to be. Reaching over, he placed his hand in hers and just stared, as she slept peacefully in the chair next to his bed.

Chapter 18

A cute little cottage house with a white picket fence, a swing set in the backyard, a bike lying on its side in the driveway. Charlotte stands on the corner of her property, just taking it all in as Brooks pushes their daughter on the swings and their son kicks a ball into the soccer net. Their golden retriever chasing after the ball makes her laugh. She looks up and meets Brooks's smile. The love shining in his eyes was hard to miss. She's startled when she feels a hand slip into her own. Looking down, she sees nothing...

She slowly opened her eyes, shaking off the dream, a small part of her wishing it were true. As her eyes focused, it took a few minutes to remember why she was in an uncomfortable chair in a hospital room. Her head whipped toward the bed when she felt a gentle squeeze in her hand.

"Hi," Brooks croaked.

"Hey," she let out in a rush, so happy to see him awake. He had been in and out of it since she arrived a few hours ago. Mostly just blinking his eyes but never talking or making any other movements. "When did you wake up?"

"Just a couple of minutes ago. You looked so peaceful I didn't want to wake you."

His voice was hoarse. Grabbing the water from his tray, she poured him a cup and pressed it to his lips. Using his good arm, he reached up and took the cup from her.

"Don't be silly. I was only taking a quick cat nap while everyone grabbed food. You should have woken me up."

She was relieved to hear him talking. It had taken her a while to convince his family to step away, even for ten minutes. She had laid her head down just moments after they left to gather her strength, not even realizing she fell asleep until she started dreaming. And what a nice dream it was.

He simply shrugged with his good shoulder as he lifted his lips in a smirk.

"What are you doing here?"

The bluntness of his question stung. Chalking it up to pain and just waking up, she shrugged it off before responding.

"I'm here because you got shot. Where else would I be?"

"I didn't mean it like that," he rasped, clearing his throat. "I'm glad you're here. Just surprised."

"Gee, thanks. You make me sound like a lousy friend," she laughed humorlessly.

There was nothing funny about what happened, but it was either that, or she was going to lose it. She had to stop herself several times from bursting into tears, especially as she watched Leslie and his mother crying when she first arrived. It had taken everything in her power not to join them. But it wasn't her place. She was simply the friend who had flown all the way from Boston, and no one really understood why. And she couldn't tell them it was because she was in love with their son. Hell, she had just realized it herself on the plane and she was too busy freaking the fuck out about it to fully process what it meant. Plus, she figured if anyone should hear about it first, it would be Brooks.

"I'm sorry, that wasn't how I meant it," he apologized once again.

Before she could respond, the door cracked open, and a stunning brunette peeked her head in.

"Oh hey, you're awake. Your mother said you were still sleeping."

"Hey, Abby. Come on in. I just woke up a few minutes ago."

Using one arm, Brooks propped himself higher in the bed. She moved to help him, but he waved her off.

So, this was Abby, the woman he had gone through the academy with. A spark of jealousy hit her in the chest. When he had first told her about the woman, she had thought nothing of it. She was just another police officer. But now, seeing her out of uniform and standing in Brooks's room, was something entirely different. Hadn't he said something about them dating at one point? Or maybe it was just one date.

You should have paid more attention, dumbass. Then you wouldn't have to look desperate when you ask him.

And she would ask. She wasn't the type of woman who got jealous, so that alone was pissing her off, but it was also the principle of the matter. She didn't do drama and loving a man who might still be in love with his partner was not okay.

She was so lost in her thoughts that she didn't realize the two of them were trying to speak to her. Now they were both staring at her with concerned looks on their faces. Groaning, she thought, *How long have they been staring at me?*

"Sorry I was lost in thought. What did you say?"

"I was just introducing you to Abby," Brooks replied with a perplexed look on his face.

"So, you're Charlotte, the woman Brooks can't stop talking about," Abby said, thrusting her hand forward for a shake. "It's so good to finally meet you. I've heard a lot about you."

"Hopefully, most of it's good." She tried for a laugh but again her heart wasn't in it.

What had he told this woman? It wasn't like they had the best start. She did run off after screwing around with him in the woods without so much as a goodbye or a way to call her. She winced at the memory. Yeah, she could only imagine what was said.

"Mostly," Abby giggled. It sounded like a true laugh and Charlotte didn't sense any resentment or bad feelings. Maybe there wasn't anything to worry about between them. Damn, she didn't want to be the jealous type.

Again, a knocking at the door interrupted her reply. Not that she really had one. For the first time in her life, she was speechless. This was certainly not something she knew how to cope with.

"Oh good, you're awake."

This time it was Brooks's mother and father. As his mother cracked the door open wider, Charlotte could see the rest of the family just outside. Well, everyone except for

Rhett. He was deployed and unable to get leave. Leslie had shared that tidbit during one of her many pregnancy-induced emotional rantings while they waited.

Wanting to give the family some time with their son, she excused herself and stepped out into the hallway. Leaning against the wall, she slowly slid down until her ass hit the floor. With her knees bent up to her chest, she wrapped her arms around her legs and put her head down. She ignored it when the door opened again. She watched as a shadow passed by but stopped just inches away. A moment later she tilted her head to the side. Her eyes locking with Abby's brilliant green ones.

"It was getting crowded in there and I felt like an intruder. His family should have their alone time."

She knew exactly what Abby meant. It was the same reason she had excused herself.

"Did you and Brooks actually date?" she blurted out before she could stop herself. She hadn't stopped thinking about it and had every intention of asking Brooks at a different time, but it would appear her mouth had its own agenda.

Of course, it did, you have no damn filter.

Abby chuckled. "Straight to the point. I like that. And to answer your question, no. Well, not really. He asked me out once, but about halfway through drinks, we realized there was absolutely no chemistry. I see him more as a brother."

Good, because he's mine, she wanted to scream, but fortunately, her self-control was back even for just a moment. She could only manage a nod.

"Besides, in case you haven't already figured it out, he's totally into you. I wasn't exaggerating when I said he hasn't stopped talking about you. It's nonstop, FYI. Almost gag-worthy. I would be freaked out if I didn't think it was kinda adorable. A girl would kill to have a man that interested in her. I mean, I know I would."

"Yeah, well, I figured he probably didn't have a lot of nice things to say in the beginning." She cringed.

"Oh, trust me, I wanted to kick your ass in the beginning. I was completely on the team 'forget Charlotte ever existed,' but then I saw the way he changed when he came back from Boston and how happy he's been these last few months. I can tell when your name pops up, he gets this stupid happy grin on his face. I would make fun of him for it but I'm just glad it's there."

She didn't know what to say. And she didn't get the chance before Abby said, "And fair warning. You hurt him and there isn't a place you can hide that I won't find you and kill you."

The smile with which she delivered her speech was scarier than the words themselves. She believed the woman.

"Duly noted. But just to be clear, I have no intention of hurting him. The opposite in fact."

She left it at that. Brooks deserved to hear how she felt first. But it was clear by the look in Abby's eyes that she understood what she meant.

Chapter 19

He watched as Charlotte slid out of the room followed by Abby. He wished she would stay. Not Abby. As much as he enjoyed her company and banter, it was Charlotte's hand he wanted to still be holding. For those few minutes, he had been calm.

"We're really happy you're awake. We were starting to get worried." His mother sniffled as she took a seat on the lower half of his bed.

"He was probably too busy dreaming about his girlfriend," Garrett joked.

If only his brother knew. His face must have given him away because he caught the knowing smirk on Leslie's face. Giving him a wink, she leaned into his other brother, her husband.

"Stop teasing your brother," his mother chided.

He threw Garrett a childish giggle for getting in trouble, and his mother slapped both of them after Garrett threw back the middle finger. Feeling properly chastised, Garrett apologized for his behavior.

Raising six children, four of which were boys, meant his mother stopped taking their shit a long time ago. She wasn't afraid to slap them upside the head when the need arose. She had long perfected the move before Gibbs and DiNozzo.

"There are a lot of people who will be glad to know you're awake. The waiting room is filled with fellow officers, not to mention the ones outside the hospital. It's truly amazing to see the amount of support," his father choked out.

Travis Lynch wasn't what one would call an emotional man. Having served in the Army himself, he held his children, especially his sons, to a higher expectation. It was probably the reason every one of them chose a life that served others. It was how they were raised. So to see his father now, showing emotion over what happened, really put the whole thing into perspective. He had gotten lucky.

It had taken a few minutes after waking up to have some of his memories start flooding his brain. He didn't remember it all, but bits and pieces had flashed in his head, including the dreaded *officer down* radio transmission. He could remember hearing gunshots and the way his chest and shoulder felt. He assumed he was the recipient of those shots.

"Do they have any information about the shooter?" He wanted to change the subject. While he recognized the scare it must have given his family, he wanted to focus on the fact that he was alive and that the person responsible was being sought.

"There's a lot of talk happening and a few of the officers were saying it wasn't random. That it was someone from a past incident. I don't know how true it is though," his father explained carefully. So he was right. He was indeed shot.

Brooks got the feeling his father knew more than he was willing to share in front of the rest of the family, so he wouldn't call him out on it now. There would be time later to get all the details. He would be expected to make a statement at some point, and he could ask a lot of questions then. Hopefully, whichever detective was working the case would have the answers he wanted. In the meantime, he would try to think back through his time and see if there was anyone who stuck out. Seven years was a long time, and although the goal was never to make enemies, there were times that people weren't happy with how a situation ended. Particularly if it resulted in jail time.

A knock on the door brought him back to the present. With a nod to Zack to let whoever it was in, he repositioned himself in the bed. He had started to slip down again and didn't want to look slouched. It was a good thing he did when he noticed who came through the door. His captain entered first, followed by another man in a suit, most likely the detective, but it wasn't one he had worked with before.

"Sir." He put his hand out to shake as they approached his bed.

"Glad to see you're okay, Officer Lynch," his captain replied. Turning toward the other man, he introduced Detective Matthew Daniels.

His family slid back out of the room. The next hour was spent reviewing what happened. Since he couldn't remember all of the details, it took time to compare what he did remember to witness statements and his body cam footage.

"So, you already know who shot me?"

"We believe so," his captain started. "We have a face but still running his name. Do you recognize this individual?"

Detective Daniels handed over the picture taken from his body cam. He didn't recognize the person, and just like when they asked him particular questions about the call, he couldn't remember the interaction. It was frustrating. He was normally good with faces, so he felt comfortable saying he had never met the person before.

He shook his head before handing the picture back. There was some silent communication before his captain asked, "Are you sure? From the footage we watched, it was clear he knew you. He called you by your full name. Claimed you were the reason she died. We're looking into the 'she' he was referring to."

That shocked him. He couldn't place a single incident where he was the reason a woman died. Certainly not intentionally. And he was pretty sure that was something he would remember, at least he hoped so. He never wanted to be the type of person who disregarded human life. He became a police officer because he wanted to help people. To protect and serve was in his blood. He knew himself, and if he had caused harm in any way, he would have felt compelled to leave the profession.

"I'm sure." He hesitated. "I mean I don't recognize him, but I also can't remember the moments leading up to the incident. The last thing I remember was responding to the call. After that, it's just bits and pieces like we've discussed."

"The doctor said that's common. She expects the memories to slowly return and advised us not to push them. You hit your head pretty good when you hit the ground."

That would explain the dull headache when he first woke up and its growing intensity the more he tried to pull those memories out. He would be sure to ask the doctor about that.

"Knock, knock." Speak of the devil. A middle-aged woman whose voice he recognized from the few times he went in and out of consciousness, peeked her head in the door. "I hate to interrupt but I need to examine Officer Lynch. You're more than welcome to stay."

"We'll get out of your way." His captain stepped back. "Brooks, I'll keep you posted." Both men left after a brief nod to the doctor.

"Normally, I would apologize for having guests scurry out, but I had the nurse monitoring your vitals and I could tell whatever discussion they were having was disturbing you."

The name on her coat read Dr. Montgomery. He detected a little bit of a northern accent, similar to what he noticed when he spoke to Charlotte, or Leslie before she moved back.

"I appreciate it. I'm having some difficulties remembering exactly what happened."

"That's completely normal. Your body went through a lot of trauma in the past twenty-four hours. You have a mild concussion from when you fell. You were shot and then underwent surgery to remove the bullet. It got lodged in a bone, in case you were wondering. So it's expected to be missing some memories, but I'm confident they will return soon." She smiled.

Her smile reminded him of his mother when she cared for them as young boys. Especially when they got sick.

"I hope so," he mumbled.

The doctor continued to check him over. Shining a light in his eyes and probing both his head and shoulder to see how everything felt. Surprisingly, it was better than he expected. That was, until it came time to look at the bruising on his chest. That was probably what hurt the worst. His vest certainly did its job; he was alive after all.

Finally, after all the poking and prodding, the doctor admitted that as long as he didn't show any problems, he would be discharged the following morning. He sighed with relief. No one in their right mind wanted to spend any more time than needed in the hospital.

After the doctor left, his family returned. The concern was evident on their faces. He had no idea how much they heard. None of them would admit to eavesdropping but he wouldn't put it past them. If for any other reason than they were concerned for him.

"My captain confirmed that they do suspect it was personal and not a random act," he blurted out. Better to get it out in the open. Secrets were pretty much nonexistent in a family their size. That's not to say they didn't each have a few but rarely something major.

"Do they know who?" Zack asked with a scowl, going into full sniper mode.

"They have the picture from my body cam, but I don't recognize him. They're in the process of trying to identify him."

"I'll see if my team can be given access." Zack moved back out of the room, his phone already up to his ear. Brooks wasn't given the chance to say thank you or even acknowledge the help.

"If it's personal, do you think it's safe to go back to your place alone? You can come to stay with us. I know your brother wouldn't mind," Leslie offered, wringing her hands against her belly.

He appreciated the offer but there was no way he was going to bring his mess to Zack's doorstep. It didn't matter if his company specialized in it or not, Leslie was pregnant and the last thing he wanted was for her to be in the middle if someone was after him. No one would be safe, and that included Charlotte. As much as he loved that she dropped everything to come down, there was no chance in hell he was letting her stay.

"He might not but I would. Not while you're carrying my little niece or nephew. That goes for Charlotte as well. I don't want her anywhere near me while this guy is still loose."

"Don't you think that should be her choice?" Leslie challenged.

Her hands were no longer fidgeting. Instead, they were planted firmly on her hips, disapproval rolling off her in waves. He expected some blowback when he spoke to Charlotte but not from Leslie. He had been so sure that she would be on his side.

"Not when it's her safety we're discussing," he calmly threw back, but Leslie wasn't having any of it. From the corner of his eye, he could see his family shifting. Some were clearly on his side, but if the scowls were an indication, a couple of them were backing up Leslie on this.

"She's going to argue."

"I expect as much," he sighed. Charlotte was anything but easy, but he would be able to convince her it was best. He needed to protect her.

Leslie didn't look any more convinced when Zack returned a few moments later, Charlotte at his side.

"Wes is going to see what he can find out."

He nodded to his brother but never took his eyes off Charlotte. In only leggings and a shirt, she was still the most beautiful woman he had ever laid his eyes on. All the more reason he needed to convince her she was safer away from him.

His father cleared his throat. "How about we give you two a few minutes?" he said, ushering a confused Zack and a pissed Leslie out the door, along with the rest of his family. Stopping in the doorway, his mother turned back to look at him. With a smile that didn't quite reach her eyes, she blew him a kiss, just like she had done since he was a little boy.

Charlotte watched his family leave, her eyes squinted in confusion. "What was that all about? Normally I at least have to say something to get that many people to scurry away."

Sometimes it was better just to rip the Band-Aid off. With a sigh, he looked down at his hands.

"It appears the shooting wasn't random. My captain thinks it was personal and they haven't caught the guy yet, so...it's not safe to be around me."

"So make it safe. You have a brother whose team literally does that for a living in case you've forgotten."

Lifting his head, he argued, "No, I haven't forgotten, and I don't need my little brother to keep me safe. I just don't need to worry about other people getting hurt because they're around me."

"As in your family, or me?" Charlotte folded her arms across her chest.

"Both," he murmured.

"I'm going to chalk this nonsense up to your head injury rather than the overbearing asshole you sound like." Her tone was like ice. He expected her to be spitting mad, but the ice was even worse.

"Overbearing asshole? Really?" he huffed. "Me wanting to make sure you're safe makes me an overbearing asshole?"

Charlotte certainly didn't disappoint. He expected an argument and that was exactly what she was giving him.

"Yes, it does." There was no hesitation, no reconsidering. Her raised eyebrows were a clear indication she was challenging his logic.

If she wouldn't listen to reason, then he would try another tactic.

"What about work? You've told me a thousand times that you wouldn't let a man be the reason you moved."

"Who said anything about moving? I'm entitled to vacation and that's exactly what I'm taking. Besides, last time I checked, you aren't just any man. You are a friend, and I would be doing the exact same thing if it were Leslie lying in that bed."

There really wasn't anything he could say against that, but he tried anyway.

"Go back to Boston. I would rather you there than here with me."

He probably should have demanded she left or said how he didn't want her there, but he couldn't be that mean. No matter how much he wanted her safe, he wouldn't do it at the expense of hurting her. He was a goner.

"Well, it's a good thing I'm too stubborn to listen to what you want," she casually tossed out before charging out the door.

She had gotten in the last word, and he expected she would get her way. Although he would fight like hell because he cared that much. It seemed all he did was fight for Charlotte. Fight to have her and fight to keep her safe.

Chapter 20

S he continued stomping down the hallway.

Overbearing, bossy, arrogant, cocky son of a bitch. What other words can I come up with for the asshole?

There were probably more synonyms but her pissed-off brain couldn't think of them at the moment. All that reading she did and yet not one good insult could be found. She was disappointed in herself.

Lost in her thoughts she almost ran right into Leslie who was pacing back and forth at the other end of the hallway.

"Did he kick you out?" Leslie was in mama bear mode, ready to attack whoever had the nerve to upset her best friend. It was clear by the scowl on her face. Any other time, Charlotte would be cracking up at the sight and cheering her friend on.

Side note: If the two of us ever got arrested, it would be because my stupid mouth would be encouraging the bad behavior. That thought did make her chuckle a bit.

"What's so funny?" Pregnancy made for a testy best friend.

"The way my mind works sometimes," she answered with a shrug. "And to answer your question, no, he didn't kick me out per se. I stormed out when Mr. I-think-I-know-best tried to tell me to go back to Boston."

"I *knew* you wouldn't give in." Leslie triumphantly pounded her fist against her other hand. "Do I know my best friend or what?" She turned to Zack with a glimmer in her eyes.

To Charlotte, she said, "I was just explaining to Zack what transpired while he left to call his boss."

"He probably just thinks it will be safer for you," Zack tried to reason.

"That's exactly what he said, but I call bullshit. I wouldn't run if it were Leslie and I sure as hell am not going to just because he demands it." She examined her nails. A woman's universal sign that she was done with the conversation.

"The two of you are both equally stubborn," Zack chuckled. "I might just stay for the entertainment."

Slowly lifting her head, she scowled. It didn't seem to affect him in the slightest because he continued to chuckle at her.

I must be getting rusty. I'll have to fix that.

Leslie smacked him in the chest instead. As usual, her best friend had her back. Faking surprise, Zack rubbed the spot Leslie hit, trying to keep the smirk off his face.

"While watching them fight it out sounds fun and all, can we be serious for a minute? If Charlotte wants to stay, then it should be her choice," Leslie chided her husband.

"I'm not disagreeing with you. I would never do such a thing." Charlotte snorted at his attempt to placate his wife.

He gave her the side-eye before continuing on. "But I would do the same thing in his position. I would want you safe, and if that meant away from me, then so be it." Pulling Leslie into his side, he finished in a softer tone, "Pretty sure that's exactly what you did when you left Texas."

Charlotte watched the exchange, she felt like an interloper, but the conversation was about her after all.

"It's not the same and you know it," Leslie shot back. "I was too young to realize what a mistake I was making. Brooks would be making a big mistake pushing Charlotte away now."

The conversation was beginning to feel like she was no longer a part of it. Wanting to make sure they realized she was still there, she raised her hand.

"Charlotte's still here," she said, referring to herself in the third person.

Both of them turned her way shocked, almost like they actually forgot she was still in the hallway with them. *Jerks.*

"He'll come around," Leslie assured her.

She wasn't worried about that. The only way she was going back to Boston was if someone drugged and kidnapped her. She was pretty positive Brooks wouldn't resort to those measures, but just to be safe, she would be prepping her own meals and drinks for the duration.

She changed the subject. "Are you guys staying in town?"

"Yes. The plan was to sleep at Brooks's place tonight and decide tomorrow once he got home what we'll do after that," Zack answered.

"Perfect. I'll just make myself comfortable at his place. I'm curious to see how he lives anyway."

Zack and Leslie exchanged looks. She could imagine the silent conversation went something along the lines of "It's official. She's ready for the loony bin." They wouldn't be wrong. She had to be crazy to want to stay somewhere where she wasn't wanted, but deep down she knew that was a lie. Brooks did want her around because he truly cared for her. So much so that he was willing to chance pushing her away just to keep her safe. She needed to prove that it wasn't necessary. She wasn't some damsel in distress who needed saving. She was stubborn, sassy, and anyone who tried to kidnap her would likely return her in a heartbeat because she wouldn't shut up.

"Are you heading out to Brooks's place now?" Mrs. Lynch asked as she approached. Charlotte was so busy in her own thoughts that she hadn't noticed the rest of his family had joined them.

"Yeah, we were just discussing that. Charlotte will be staying there as well," Zack informed the group.

"Good. My son needs someone who is going to challenge him."

Every one of Brooks's brothers' jaws dropped at their mother's declaration. Only the women and their father looked amused at the statement.

"Don't look at me like that. I would say it about any of you. You boys need women who will stand up to you when you're being hard-headed. How do you think your father and I survived all these years? Certainly not by being meek," she declared.

A slow smile spread across Charlotte's face. She had known from the beginning she liked Mrs. Lynch, but she didn't realize how much until this moment. The woman was her hero. She wished her own mother had the same mindset.

"I wouldn't mind meek," Garrett mumbled.

Mrs. Lynch snorted. "You, more than anyone, need someone who will put you in your place."

Garrett looked shocked. Lucy and Alexa chuckled while the rest of them just shook their heads. Zack certainly hadn't chosen meek when he married Leslie, and from what Charlotte had seen, Alexa was far from it. Whoever Alexa met would have their hands full. The only one she couldn't get a good read on was Lucy, Brooks's older sister. She wouldn't describe her as shy but she seemed more distant than the rest of her siblings. Especially when her husband was around. It was almost like she was playing a role. That or she just needed to spend more time with the woman.

"Glad we cleared that up," Mr. Lynch chuckled. There was no empathy in the man's voice. It was clear he agreed with his wife about what his sons needed. Maybe because he saw himself in them. A question to ask Brooks later.

"I know Lucy and Garrett are traveling back tonight since they both have work tomorrow, but what about you, Alexa?"

"I'll either crash at home or Garrett's since Brooks's place will be full. Doesn't bother me one bit." The youngest shrugged to her father.

Charlotte remembered Brooks mentioning that Alexa was a free spirit. She had no place of her own. She was often gone for weeks on end, and when she showed back up, she stayed with whoever had a room available. Brooks never seemed to mind, and from the nod Garrett just gave, he didn't either.

"Your mother and I plan to stay the night here but everyone else should go get some rest. We'll let you know what time he's being released."

Hugs were given all around. Brooks's parents went back down the hall towards his room. As much as she wanted to go say goodbye, it was best she just slipped out. She didn't have it in her to argue again and nothing he said would change her mind.

She followed the rest of the group out to the parking garage. With another round of see you laters, they split off into separate directions. Alexa would be riding back with Garrett. Lucy drove up on her own, and since she took a taxi from the airport, she hopped into Zack's new SUV.

"When did you get rid of the Jeep?"

"I started looking after the wedding. The Jeep was for single me, not dad me. Especially since I'm shooting for a few more after this one." His hand shot out and rubbed Leslie's nonexistent baby bump.

"How about we get through one before we start talking about more?" It was hard to miss the side-eye her friend gave. Charlotte wasn't positive but she imagined it was followed by a roll of the eyes.

Zack's only response was a shit-eating grin from ear to ear.

The city traffic wasn't as heavy this late in the evening, but it still took a while before they pulled into the little suburban neighborhood that, as Zack explained, Brooks moved into after wanting to get out of a downtown apartment. She knew from their conversations that Brooks lived in a quiet neighborhood, but she never expected it to be so family oriented. Every house they drove by had some type of kid toy in the front yard or a swing set could be seen in the backyard.

Brooks had mentioned he wanted kids. And not just one. He had similar thoughts to his brother as to the amount he wanted running around. That conversation had actually led to their first friend argument, sort of. If that's what she wanted to call it. She had been so thrown off by the conversation that she had not spoken to him for a full day. Mostly because she never really thought about it and didn't like where her mind had gone at the time. So instead, she stepped away for the day and, when he had asked about it, she played it off as having a busy day.

Was this why he had brought it up? Did he already have his life planned and was just waiting on the right woman to move in? Did he think I was the right woman? The better question is, do I want to be that woman?

The answer to that was a big question mark. Just because she was ready to admit she had feelings for him, didn't mean she was ready for the whole white dress and two-point-five-kids lifestyle.

Her thoughts changed from weddings and kids to houses the moment they pulled into Brooks's driveway. The house was cute. It was gray with blue shutters and a door to match. A small porch ran along the front of the house, with a porch swing off to one side. She pictured herself swinging on a chilly night with a cup of hot cocoa in her hand.

"Here's the key. Make yourselves at home while I bring in the bags." Zack handed a set of keys to Leslie. Following her up the stone path to the porch, they unlocked the door, and Charlotte got her first view of how Brooks lived.

The front door led into the living room with a staircase on the right wall. As expected for a single man, there was a gigantic flat screen on the one wall, but that was the end of the bachelor pad vibe she thought he would have. A large sofa took up the opposite wall from the front of the house. Throw pillows and a blanket were arranged nicely and the coffee table in the center was devoid of any clutter.

Taking her shoes off, she placed them on the rack next to the door and moved farther into the house. On the other side of the living room wall was the dining room with the kitchen off to the left. A wraparound counter separated the space. Moving around the kitchen she noticed once again the lack of clutter. Even the large dining room table was arranged as if it were for show. Either Brooks was a clean freak or he got lucky that today was the day a cleaning lady was scheduled to show up.

Leslie let out a low whistle as she accompanied Charlotte in the kitchen. "Zack wasn't kidding. The man really does keep a clean place."

Well, that answered that question. "I was beginning to think he had a fantastic cleaning lady and I was going to ask for her number."

"Nope, he just likes everything in its place," Zack added as he joined them, dropping their bags on the dining room table, shifting the properly placed settings. "Brooks's room is that way." He pointed towards the other side of the dining room. "You can sleep in there. We will take the guest room upstairs. There is another bedroom, but he's turned that into a gym of sorts."

"I'll just make myself at home." Grabbing her bag from the table, she moved in the direction Zack had pointed.

The bedroom was easy enough to find as the only other door led to a small bathroom/laundry room combo. The bedroom was exactly what she expected after seeing other parts of the house. Other than a large bed, there were only two other pieces of furniture. A tall dresser with a smaller TV on top and a nightstand on what she guessed was his dominant side to sleep. She placed her bag on the bed.

With her curiosity piqued, she began opening drawers. A lot could be said about how a person organized their clothes. Brooks appeared to be a fan of first separating by style and then color. He had a different drawer for the things he couldn't hang up and his closet closely represented a department store rack. Shirts were all hung up the same way, even the hangers looked to be spaced out exactly the same. She was beginning to worry this obsession was just a tad extreme. She was almost afraid to touch anything.

"Settling in okay?" Leslie poked her head in through the door.

"Yeah, but I'm a little concerned by the level of organization Brooks has. I mean I'm not messy, but this is over the top." She gestured to the room and closet.

"Yeah, I'm a bit surprised as well. I wish Zack had even half of Brooks's cleanliness. I would be happy if he at least put his clothes in the laundry basket rather than on the floor," Leslie chuckled.

That was exactly the type of thing she had expected to find when she showed up. Or at least mail on the counter. Simple things that most people didn't even think of when they left for work. Maybe there was a hidden drawer or closet that everything got shoved in. She just needed to explore more.

"Well, if you're all good, then we're heading to bed. I'm exhausted and Zack promised me a nice back rub."

"You kids have fun. I'm just going to grab a quick shower and then I'll be crashing myself."

"Okay. Night."

"Night." She waved Leslie off.

Grabbing a change of clothes from her bag, she walked into the bathroom. For a master bath, it wasn't large. The sink was outside the actual bathroom area, across from the closet. On one side was a tub/shower combo and the other was the toilet and what appeared to be a linen closet. Her assumption was correct when she opened the door and found a stack of blue towels. The man sure was a fan of sticking to one color. Almost everything she had noticed was some shade of blue with the occasional gray thrown in. Even the walls had a hint of blue.

Turning on the shower, she sat on the floor while she waited for the water to warm up. Had it really been just that morning that she had woken up to Leslie's insistent call, letting her know Brooks had been shot? She had taken the first flight out but hadn't arrived until close to noon. It was hours later before he finally woke up and now here she was almost twenty hours after receiving the call, sitting on the floor, bone-tired and ready to sleep. But first, she needed to clean up, and then she could crawl into Brooks's bed and fall asleep to his scent knowing he was safe.

Chapter 21

He hated hospitals. That wasn't true, but after that morning, he could understand why people did hate them. It had taken forever to get his discharge paperwork. Then he had to promise them his firstborn child that he would attend therapy otherwise it would take longer to return to work. He loved his job and wouldn't do anything to jeopardize his road to recovery. Which was exactly what he told the nurse after the millionth time she reminded him of his first appointment.

Now he was finally on his way back to his house and all he wanted was some alone time. Not that he expected to get it. His parents were the ones driving him back and he knew for a fact Zack and Leslie were staying in his guest room. Secretly, he hoped Charlotte had returned to Boston but his heart, on the other hand, wished she was there when he arrived, welcoming him back home. When did he become such a sap? And more importantly, when did he become so damn indecisive about what he wanted?

As his parents pulled into his driveway, he found exactly who he expected, waiting for him on the porch. His heart did a little flip at the stubborn set of Charlotte's jaw. That was his girl. Sassy and never a dull moment. Too bad he was going to have to convince her it was best to leave. He looked forward to the challenge. Clearing his face of all emotions, he stepped out of the vehicle and approached the porch.

"I appreciate you guys staying until I got home but I'm fine," he told the group, but was met with nothing but blank stares. "Really, there's no need for you guys to stay around. I know you all have long drives home."

"We'll leave in the morning since I have to get back for work," Zack answered, before pulling his wife back into the house, not waiting for a response.

"Your mother and I only wanted to make sure you got home, but if you need anything, please don't hesitate to call. We can come out for as long as you like," his father told him as he pulled him in for a hug.

"I promise to call if I need anything." He gave his mother a long hug. Just before he was about to pull away, she whispered in his ear.

"Don't say anything stupid you can't take back." With a kiss on his cheek, she walked back to the car. His parents waved as they drove off.

Taking a deep breath, he turned back to the only other person left. Before he could even open his mouth to speak, she beat him to it.

"I wasn't kidding when I said I wasn't leaving."

Looks like we're doing this now.

"And I wasn't kidding when I said it wasn't safe for you to be here," he growled back.

Crossing her arms over her chest, she didn't back down. "Well, then, I guess you better find a way to make it safe for me because I'm not going anywhere." Turning on her heel, she stomped back into the house, leaving him alone with his thoughts.

Why did she have to challenge him? But an even better question was, why did he get turned on by it? Instead of being upset that she wasn't leaving, he looked forward to their future banter. There was something wrong with him mentally. With a sigh, he followed her inside.

It wasn't until he entered his living room that he felt self-conscious. This was the first time someone other than his family was seeing the way he lived. Abby knew about his obsessiveness for order, but what did Charlotte think of how he lived? His family thought it was a bit extreme, but since he had been the same way since he was a kid, they were used to it. Girlfriends in the past just assumed he straightened up before they came over and he never bothered to correct them. But this time was different. He hadn't planned to get shot at work or for Charlotte to visit, so there was no way to hide that he lived this way all the time.

The thought had never bothered him before but suddenly he wished he had left a piece of mail out or maybe even his shoes by the entryway. Something so he looked like a normal guy.

"Why are you fighting her so hard on this? We all see the way you look at her," Zack asked from his position on the couch. There was no sign of Leslie or Charlotte.

Dropping onto the other side of the couch, he made sure not to jostle his shoulder. It was in a sling for a few days until he started therapy. Then they would decide how much longer he needed to wear it.

"That's exactly why I don't want her here. I do care. More than a friend probably should." That was the most he was going to say about it until he had the chance to speak to Charlotte. "If it were Leslie, you would want her out of harm's way as well."

"And that is where you're wrong, brother. I have learned to respect my wife's opinion. If she thought she could handle it, then I would do everything in my power to make that so. I have an entire team who would be willing to help. Just say the word."

The idea grated on his nerves. He didn't want to be dependent on anyone to keep Charlotte safe but him. It should be his job and it wasn't like he wasn't trained to do just that. But something about the whole situation was bothering him and he couldn't put his finger on it.

"I don't need the help. I just don't like not knowing. What I need is my memory to come back," he groaned.

He had been trying to remember since he woke up but all it did was give him a headache. His doctor had advised him it was best to let them come back on their own, but he wasn't patient. He wanted them back now, or better yet, yesterday, when he woke up and his captain showed him the picture. He wanted to remember what the guy had meant when he said he was the reason for death, what it meant for his future and possibly Charlotte's.

"Suit yourself, but don't let your ego get in the way." Zack pushed off from the couch and moved towards the dining room, stopping to say, "As for the memories, stop forcing them. They'll come when they're most needed. Now I need to figure out where my wife ran off to. She followed Charlotte after she stormed through earlier."

The smirk on his brother's face was enough to make him want to punch the man. The women were probably cursing him up and down and plotting a way to get their revenge. Leslie didn't seem like the type to plan long term, but Charlotte sure did. It was probably best if he followed. Even if it was to ensure they weren't planning his death.

He found them out back on the patio. After attending Zack and Leslie's wedding at Wes's cabin, he had the itch to turn his backyard into an oasis. He had gotten as far as putting in a fire pit area with several chairs before life got too busy. He kept meaning to hire out rather than do the work himself, but something always came up.

Maybe you were waiting until a certain someone could give you their opinion on it.

He shut down the voice that liked to remind him that having only a friendship with Charlotte was such bullshit it was almost comical. Just when he thought he was getting better with the idea, that nagging voice would remind him he wanted more, and if he wasn't such a bitch about it, he would tell her.

"If you're coming out here just to argue, you can march your fine ass back in the house right now," Charlotte sassed him.

"Fine ass, huh?"

"I meant stubborn ass." The tops of her cheeks held just a touch of pink.

Was that a blush? I'll be damned. She rarely blushed.

Wanting to see if he could deepen the blush, he threw back, "But you said *fine* ass."

Letting out the cutest little growl, she stomped her foot. "Argh, you're insufferable!"

As expected, the pink on her cheeks deepened with every word she spoke.

Yup, definitely blushing. I'm going to have to make that happen more often.

It would be a fun experiment to see what he could do to get her to blush. He already knew she didn't when they had sex. Well, at least not angry sex or screwing around in the woods during a wedding. So it was probably safe to assume she was either not embarrassed by those actions or there was something else going on at the moment that he was unaware of. He was tempted to try and discover what that was, but they had an audience and he doubted Leslie would appreciate that type of behavior. Also, it would be weird in front of his brother. They were close but not "I'll fuck a chick in front of you" close. That was a whole other level of brotherhood.

Giving Charlotte his most charming smile, he took a seat next to her, completely ignoring the glare she was throwing his way. But she wasn't the only one glaring. When he met his sister-in-law's eyes, she too was shooting daggers his way. While he might not mind sparring with Charlotte, he had no intention of also pissing off Leslie.

Putting his one good arm up in surrender, he apologized for his behavior. Zack simply chuckled and shook his head, Leslie looked satisfied with the apology, but Charlotte didn't seem prepared to forgive him just yet. With her arms planted firmly in her lap, she sat back in the chair. Her eyes narrowed and lips in a straight line as if she was trying to determine what game he was playing.

"I really am sorry," he leaned over and whispered.

Charlotte's shoulders sagged just a bit. It was the first sign that she was softening toward him.

"If we're going to be roommates, don't you think it would be better not to do it fighting?" He tried to sound calm, but he was anything but.

His heart was racing a million miles a minute and his palms were sweaty. He was torn between wanting to see how things went living together and pushing her away. His heart and brain were playing a damn ping-pong game, never knowing what was going to come out of his mouth or which one would win at any given moment.

"Does that mean you're finally accepting of me staying with you?"

Damn, she was challenging him again. Not wanting to lie to her, he took an extra minute to put his thoughts in order before answering.

"For now." A smug smile broke out on her face. "But only until I get more information. If at any point I find it's no longer safe, I will personally put you on a plane back to Boston."

Her smile dropped a bit, and he could see the wheels turning behind her eyes. She was formulating a response or a plan, but instead, she simply nodded. He had no idea what that nod meant. Did she agree with him? Or was she just placating him for now? Damn, why did the woman have to be so complicated?

She completely threw him off when she asked her next question.

"So, are you going to throw me out if I hang up a towel the wrong way or leave a fork in the sink?"

Her face was so serious that all he could do was throw his head back and roar with laughter. Leslie and Zack who had been oblivious to their conversation looked over, both with their eyebrows raised. It was several moments before he got his laughter under control enough to speak.

"No, I won't throw you out. You should see what the place looks like when Alexa stays for a few days. I pride myself on keeping the place tidy, but I won't freak out if it's not."

"But even your closet is overly organized," she argued.

"It is. I like MY stuff that way, but I don't expect others to be the same way. As long as you're not a total slob, I think we'll be fine."

From the corner of his eye, he could see the smirk on his brother's face. If he wasn't too busy trying to watch Charlotte's face so closely for any signs she didn't believe what he was saying, he would have asked what the smirk was for. But he was more concerned with Charlotte. Her normally confident demeanor was gone. She was nibbling on the corner of her mouth, making him think she was dissecting what he said.

"What is it?" There was obviously something bothering her, but he was used to her speaking her mind. He rarely had to ask.

"Nothing," she said, too quickly. "Just wondering if I got in over my head is all."

Now it was his turn to frown. Pulling his chair closer to hers, he whispered, "What do you mean?"

"Was I too pushy? About staying? About you letting me stay? About everything?"

Each sentence was another jab to his heart. He was the reason this confident and strong woman was questioning herself and that hurt.

"No," he answered in all seriousness. "No, you weren't too pushy. I let my worry for you cloud the fact that I should be embracing this time with you."

"As friends," she interjected.

"Right." His heart broke. "As friends."

For a second there he had thought they were on the same page, that she had developed more feelings for him than just friends, but it seemed he was wrong. Giving her a weak smile, he turned away.

Chapter 22

Okay, that was meant to be a question, not a statement. She had wanted to see if they were on the same page, but apparently, they weren't.

I'm such an idiot.

Now it made sense why he was pushing so hard for her to leave. He didn't want her cramping his style. She would have to look for flights out tomorrow. In the meantime, she would do everything in her power to make sure she wasn't an extra burden to him. He needed to heal after all.

Brooks cleared his throat next to her. With his attention focused on Zack and Leslie, she took the opportunity to just look at him. Since the moment they met, their life together had been a roller-coaster ride of emotions. She remembered the first time she laid eyes on him. Sexy. That was the word that had popped into her head. It was still true, but now after months of talking to him, she also knew he was funny and smart. A little quirky sometimes, but over all his sexiness only grew the more she learned.

Staring at his profile she thought about his chiseled jaw and how the stubble felt brushing against her sensitive lips as he lapped her up in the woods. Or the way the little dent in his chin jutted out when he threw his head back and screamed her name. Just the thoughts of their encounters had her panting with need. Realizing they weren't alone, she shut down the memories for a later date. Like when she was back in Boston in her own bed.

I don't actually need a man after all. I have Bob and plenty of book boyfriends.

Zack cleared his throat, bringing her attention back to the fact that they were all still sitting in Brooks's backyard.

"Ummm, Leslie and I had a question for the two of you." His tone was serious, something that rarely happened. Sitting up a little taller, she gave him her full attention.

"That sounds ominous," Brooks stated.

"No, it's good, we swear," Leslie chimed in. "We wanted to ask the both of you if you would consider being the baby's godparents?"

The tears pooling in Leslie's eyes had her fighting back her own. Jumping up from her chair, she lunged at her best friend. She wrapped her arms around her best friend's neck and let the tears flow freely.

"Yes! Absolutely. I would be honored," she blubbered into Leslie's neck.

She heard Zack and Brooks exchange similar words with what she figured was a clasp on the back. She didn't know for sure, since she had yet to move from her position at Leslie's side.

"You've been my best friend through every major event in my life and I couldn't imagine a better woman for the job," Leslie cried into her shoulder.

"My ride and die. Forever and always," she responded.

"Forever and always," Leslie echoed. "And I hope you're ready to hold my hand as I bring this baby into the world. Someone needs to make sure Zack stays upright."

"Hey," he yelped.

Charlotte chuckled at the thought. She had no worries that the man would do just fine. She'd heard some of the stories about his time in the military and she was sure he had seen much worse than a woman having a baby. Although, she doubted he would keep calm while Leslie was pushing the baby out. If there was one thing she had noticed about Zack, it was that he hated to see Leslie uncomfortable. He was a protector. It was entwined in his DNA, just like his brother. He would want to take the pain away from her.

They celebrated the evening by grilling some steaks and making s'mores. By the time they moved back inside, it was late. Wrapped in each other's arms, Zack and Leslie moved upstairs to the guest room. Feeling awkward, Charlotte stood in the kitchen, cleaning up the last of the dishes.

Last night she had slept in Brooks's bed while he had been at the hospital. Since arriving back home, they had yet to discuss the sleeping arrangements.

"You don't have to clean up. I can get it. Why don't you just head to bed?" Brooks said as he moved through the dining room towards her.

"It's not going to be easy with just one arm, and besides, I'm almost done. Once I'm finished, I'll grab a blanket and pillow to crash on the couch."

"Absolutely not." Brooks stopped next to her, leaning against the counter. "You can have my bed tonight. If you don't feel comfortable with me sleeping in there as well, then I'll take the couch."

Her heart stopped at the mention of them sleeping in the same bed. It's not like they hadn't slept together before. Emphasis on the word *slept*. The last time they stayed at Leslie's, they had fallen asleep on the couch together, but this was different. This would be them intentionally going to sleep in the same bed. She wasn't sure that was a good idea.

"You can't sleep on the couch with your shoulder."

"Then it's settled! We'll both sleep in the bed," he added too cheerfully.

"Do you really think that's a good idea?"

She was putting her foot in her mouth. Why couldn't she just accept what he said and move on? Instead, she had to challenge him. Just like she did every time they talked.

"Why not? It'll just be two friends sharing a bed. I'll even wear pajamas." He threw her his panty-dropping smile.

"Right," she mumbled. She knew it would be anything but. Pajamas or not, and at the moment she was disappointed that he would be wearing them, he would still be too close. No amount of just friends was going to help her sleep peacefully with him lying next to her. Trying to find an excuse, she finished cleaning up before making her way back to his bedroom.

She walked in and found him already changed for bed. As promised, he was wearing a pair of pajama bottoms, but he had yet to put on a shirt. Watching the way his abs moved as he walked around the room had her mouth watering.

How the fuck am I supposed to sleep next to a sexy man and not jump his bones?

Groaning, she grabbed her own set of pajamas from her bag and slipped into the bathroom. Turning on the shower, she decided to stall for time by rinsing off, something that was completely un-Charlotte like. If she wanted something, she would have put on skimpy pajamas and strutted around until Brooks noticed her.

But that wasn't what she wanted now. She was over mindless sex. She wanted more. And right now, more sucked. Because more was one-sided. With any hope, he would already be in bed and asleep by the time she got out there. Taking time to thoroughly brush her teeth and clean up every water droplet, she finally moved back into the bedroom.

Clearly, luck was not on her side tonight because she found a very awake Brooks sitting on the bed waiting for her.

"I was beginning to think you were going to hide in there all night," he chuckled.

"I'd considered it," she mumbled under her breath. Giving him a quick smile, she said a bit louder, "Sorry, I didn't mean to keep you from it. The bathroom is all yours." She waved rather dramatically.

"Oh, I don't need it. I was just wondering if you were ever going to come out."

"And what does that mean?" She placed her hands on her hips. She hadn't planned on fighting with him. She wanted to get through the night as smoothly as possible and then book a flight out the following day. They weren't on the same page. He wanted to continue the friends-only relationship which she could do easily enough from Boston. As long as she didn't have to *see* him every day.

"I didn't take you for someone to hide." He smiled innocently.

"I wasn't hiding." *Liar!* "I was getting ready for bed," she explained slowly.

"So, you always take that long to get ready for bed?"

Why was this even a discussion at this point?

Frustrated, she barked out, "Yes!"

No! I was hiding from you and your sexy body.

She couldn't tell him that, but she was very close to screaming it. He was flustering her, and she didn't like it. It put her on edge, and she wanted to lash out. That certainly wouldn't help the situation, so she took a calming breath instead.

"I'm tired, and I'm assuming you are as well." She rubbed her forehead. "Why don't we just get some sleep," she let out in exasperation. "Are you sure you don't want me to take the couch?"

"Nope. I'm good with sharing a bed. No reason for either of us to be uncomfortable on the small couch."

She wouldn't mind the uncomfortable couch at the moment. If it meant she didn't have to be that close to his body, she would gladly take it.

Suck it up. Put your big-girl pants on and just climb into the damn bed. You're both adults for fuck's sake.

She was talking to herself an awful lot lately. Maybe she should see someone about that. Or she was just going crazy. It sure as hell felt that way.

Not feeling much better after her little pep talk, she took a shallow breath, plastered a fake smile on her face, and climbed on the opposite side. It wasn't the same side she had slept on last night. Oh no, she had wanted to fall asleep wrapped up in his scent, so she had purposely used his pillow. Now she wished she didn't because it was going to suck trying to sleep without it.

Lying flat on her back as far on the edge as she could manage without actually falling off, she placed her palms against her stomach and looked up at the ceiling. She heard Brooks sigh before turning off the light. The bed dipped as he got himself comfortable on his own side.

"Goodnight, beautiful." It was the same thing he told her every night before they hung up. A smile touched her lips at the familiar endearment.

"Goodnight, hot stuff," she whispered back.

Turning onto her side, she propped her hands under her head. Okay, so maybe things weren't so bad after all. They could make this work. As long as she kept her feelings boxed up tight until she got back to Boston, everything would be fine. She just needed to bring back sassy Charlotte. With a smile on her face, she drifted off to sleep, completely oblivious of the turmoil currently inside Brooks.

Chapter 23

*S*tupid, stupid, stupid. Why the fuck did I think this was going to be a good idea?

Lying in bed only a few feet away from Charlotte was sweet torture. He could smell whatever soap she used. Before he realized what he was doing, he turned his head in her direction and inhaled. A hint of honey hit his nose.

Fuck. She smells as sweet as I remember.

Memories of their night in the woods slammed into his thoughts. She had smelled like honey that night as well and tasted just as sweet. He grew hard just thinking about their time together. Slowly moving his hand down his chest, he adjusted himself as quietly as he could. How awkward would it be if she turned over while he was busy trying to calm his raging hard-on? Yeah, that would certainly make her feel better about sleeping in the same bed as him. It had taken every effort he had to school his features and not let on how badly he wanted to sleep next to her. If she knew what was going on in his head, she would run for the hills.

Breathing in and out, he cleared his mind and listened for any movement from Charlotte. Her breathing had evened out a few minutes after he said goodnight, and as far as he could tell, she was asleep. Relieved that he hadn't botched everything, he turned onto his good shoulder. The doctor had recommended he sleep on his back, but he was a side or belly sleeper. He figured as long as he didn't roll onto his injury, he was fine.

Listening to Charlotte's even breaths lulled him into sleep. When he woke up again, it was to something tickling his nose. Coming fully awake, he realized the tickling was from Charlotte's hair. At some point in the night, she had moved closer and now his arm was wrapped around her middle, her ass was tucked against his erection. Shifting his head slightly, he noticed it was still dark out. Not wanting to wake her, he shifted his head slightly so her hair was no longer in his nose. Too selfish to let go of her, he drifted back to sleep.

The sun shining through the window and the feel of a perfect heart-shaped ass rubbing against his dick was how he woke up the second time. The sound of Charlotte's soft groan was enough for him to almost lose himself right there.

Shifting himself back a little to make room for his growing length, he whispered, "Morning, beautiful."

At first, she simply mumbled something he couldn't understand but he sensed the moment she fully came awake. Her body tensed seconds before she leaped out of his arms. Working hard not to show how disappointed he was, he plastered a fake smile on his face.

"What...I'm sorry...I didn't mean to...you know." She waved her hand at his dick. He wasn't entirely sure what she meant by "didn't mean to," so he raised his eyebrow without answering.

Letting out a huff, she continued, "I didn't mean to you know"—again with the hand waving but this time she added the between-them motion—"rub my ass on you while I was sleeping or get all in your space," she finally spat out.

It was too bad she hadn't meant it because truthfully, it was the best sleep he had in a while. And what guy would complain about waking up next to her? The only thing he regretted was the blue balls he was going to have if he didn't take care of himself soon. He figured suggesting that she help was not really an option. He didn't look forward to being shot down, or worse, having her throw something at him.

"Can we just forget this happened?" she pleaded.

"Already forgotten."

Liar!

He wanted to kick his subconscious ass. He hated lying. Especially to someone he cared about, but he didn't see a choice. The best he could do was try to actually forget so that it was no longer a lie. Easier said than done.

"I'm going to go grab a shower," he said, as casually as possible.

He slid off the bed and quickly turned his back towards her, hoping to hide his still-hard erection. It was one thing for her to have felt it, he could easily play it off as morning wood. But he didn't need it jutting out as he walked to the bathroom. Tucking himself into his waistband, he grabbed a pair of clean boxers and shorts before moving away.

Locking himself in the bathroom, he turned on the shower and stood just outside it. Tipping his head back he prayed for some type of control. It was clear he was lacking in that department lately. With the water hot enough to melt his skin off, he stripped down and hopped in. Without waiting, he fisted his dick and began pumping. Thoughts of Charlotte rubbing against him in her sleep was all he needed to finish. It had been months since anything other than his own hand had gotten him off.

Like the lovesick fool he was, he hadn't been with another woman since their time together in the woods. If he kept it up, he was going to shoot off like an inexperienced teenager the next time a woman finally did touch him.

No, not any woman. Charlotte. I only want Charlotte.

Reaching blindly, he grabbed his body wash, only to realize when he flipped the top it wasn't his after all. Taking in a deep breath of the honey body wash he knew Charlotte used, he leaned back against the wall and took the few moments to let the smell fill his nostrils. Looking around the shower, he noticed the few things she had added. Instead of feeling panic like he expected from having someone invade his space, he smiled. He liked having her things amongst his. It felt right. With a permanent smile, he finished cleaning up.

By the time he got back to his room, Charlotte was gone. Following her laughter, he found her in the kitchen with Zack and Leslie. Not wanting to interrupt the moment, he leaned against the wall and just watched her radiant smile. He missed that carefree smile she usually wore. At the hospital, she had been worried, and since arriving at his house, she had nothing but a scowl for him. He wanted to change that. He much preferred her the way she was now.

Sensing his presence, Zack turned in his direction.

"Awfully long shower there, brother. Having some difficulties?" The knowing smirk on his brother's face had him throwing the middle finger as he approached the fridge.

"Now, is that any way to greet your brother who is just concerned about your well-being?" Zack dramatically stated, a hand across his chest. His brother had missed his calling as an actor.

"Yup," he shot back, pulling down a glass and pouring himself orange juice.

Realizing he wasn't going to get a rise out of him, Zack simply chuckled. Meeting Leslie's gaze, he found a similar smirk on his sister-in-law's face. Luckily for him, she wasn't about to call him out on it. Finally, he turned to Charlotte who was conveniently focused on her cup of coffee, not meeting his eyes.

"So, what did I interrupt?" he asked casually.

"Zack was just explaining all the crazy ideas he had for our baby," Leslie answered. "He seems to forget that it will be months before the baby can do anything besides eat, sleep, and poop."

"What kind of crazy ideas?"

He probably shouldn't have asked but he wanted to know what Charlotte had been smiling at before she realized he was in the room. He was hoping it would return if Zack continued to talk.

"Two words. Sniper school," was all Zack said, his face was completely serious.

Spitting out his orange juice, he wiped his mouth. His brother couldn't be serious but, if his face was any indication, he absolutely was.

"You do realize that's not a 'couple of months away' thing?" he began. "That's more like another decade, if not more, kind of thing."

"Nah"—he waved his hand dismissively—"it's in the blood."

Leslie rolling her eyes was all it took for him to break out into a fit of laughter. No wonder they had been laughing so hard when he came out of his room. He had the mental image of Leslie pushing out a baby holding a rifle. Just the thought of a baby being a sniper was so damn ridiculous the only option was to laugh. He was glad to see Charlotte was laughing as well. If it wouldn't have been weird, he would have just sat back and watched her laugh. The sound alone was like music to his ears. But it would be weird, so instead, he settled for side glances, taking in his fill every chance he got.

"When do you find out the gender?" he asked.

"I go for the bloodwork next week. We opted to find out early that way. And it takes about a week to get the results back. Then it's just a matter of how we plan on announcing it," Leslie giggled.

"Screaming it from the damn rooftops!" Zack suggested.

"Or something a little less dramatic," his wife chimed in.

"Either way, I can't wait!"

The excitement in Charlotte's voice couldn't be missed. It was the same excitement she had when they were asked to be the godparents. Something he was both shocked and happy about. Especially because it meant he would get more time with Charlotte.

"We better get on the road. Wes called and said something was up and he needed me back."

"Everything okay?" Wes was Zack's boss, and he wouldn't have called if it wasn't important. Especially since this wasn't exactly a social visit.

"I'm not sure. He was super vague and Kade has yet to text me back. The fucker must be sleeping off a hangover."

Kade was the other half of the sniper team. The two had been together for so long that Brooks pretty much considered him another brother. Until Leslie, the two were inseparable, so it was strange for Kade not to be responding.

"Well, if you need anything, you know where to find me."

Hugs and goodbyes were given with promises of getting together again soon. They only lived about three hours away from each other, but between their schedules, it was often months before they hung out. Maybe it was time to change that. There was a baby on the way, after all, and he would want to be around to watch him or her grow up.

Waving from the porch, he watched as they backed out of his driveway and drove off. It suddenly dawned on him that he was alone with Charlotte.

Turning her way, with a huge smile on his face, he asked, "So what do you want to do today?"

Without looking his way, she answered, "I should probably look for flights back to Boston."

His smile faltered. With his brows dipping in, he tried to make sense of what she was saying.

"Why? I thought you wanted to stay."

"I don't want to be a burden to you or take up your space..."

This uncertainty was out of character for her, and he didn't like it. She still wouldn't look at him, so he moved until he was in front of her. Using his finger, he tipped up her chin until their eyes met.

"You could never be a burden, and I know at first I fought you, but I would like it if you stayed. At least for a few days," he confessed.

What he really wanted to say was he wished she would stay forever. Did the threat still worry him? Absolutely, but he would move heaven and earth if it meant she would be his. He had realized last night in the hospital that he had overreacted when he demanded she returned to Boston. Since then, he had come to accept that if he wanted a life with her, then it meant he would have to accept that, as a police officer, there were times where his job wasn't safe. If Zack could manage to build a life with Leslie, then he could do the same. Too bad he was still friend-zoned.

He had hoped yesterday she would clarify that she did not, in fact, want to be just friends, but that never happened. So now he was just trying to make the best of the situation. Which included convincing her to stay for a few days so he could get some extra time with her.

"Are you sure?"

Her eyes looked so sad. He wanted to banish the sadness but the only idea that came to mind was to kiss her. Figuring that wasn't the best idea, he rubbed his thumb along her cheek instead.

"Yes, I'm sure." He stared right into her eyes, hoping that they conveyed everything he wanted to say but was too afraid to.

"O...kay," she stammered.

Moving away from her at that moment was one of the hardest things he had ever done. His heart screamed to lean in and kiss her while his head argued against the notion. In the end, it was his head that won out.

"Okay, now that's settled, let's get some breakfast and decide what we're going to do for the day."

Turning on his heel, he didn't wait to see if she followed. It was probably best that she didn't. He needed a minute to calm his racing heart. It seemed to be all over the damn place lately.

Chapter 24

What the fuck just happened?

For a moment, she thought Brooks was going to kiss her on the front porch. When he didn't, her heart nearly combusted from how fast it was beating. Why did the man have to turn her mind to mush and make her belly flutter? She had thought she had everything under control when she fell asleep last night but that was blown to hell when she woke up rubbing her ass against his cock like a damn bitch in heat. Apparently, the dream she had about him had spread into the real world.

So now she was at two strikes, and it wasn't even noon. How the fuck was she supposed to spend a few days with him? She had lost her mind. That was the only explanation for agreeing to stay. Realizing she had spent too long standing on the porch arguing with herself, she moved through the house. She found Brooks in the kitchen pulling items out of the fridge.

"Can I help?"

"No, I got it. Cooking relaxes me," he told her as he cracked eggs in a bowl.

"Shouldn't you be wearing your sling?"

She didn't want to sound like a nagging wife, and she had no idea what the doctor's orders were since she wasn't there when he was released, but she figured if they sent it home with him, there was a good chance he was supposed to be wearing it.

"Yeah, but it won't hurt to have it off for a little bit. I'll put it back on after breakfast."

She accepted his answer for what it was. She would watch to make sure he didn't look to be in pain, but other than that, it was his life and she was never a fan of people telling her what to do, so she certainly wouldn't do it to someone else.

"I hope you like omelets."

"As a matter of fact, I do." She smiled.

Charlotte watched as he made breakfast, admiring how good he looked in the kitchen. There was something immensely attractive about a man who could cook. She took his distraction as an opportunity to watch him. The way his strong hands whisked the eggs. She knew from them being inside her that they weren't soft hands like a lot of the men she met. No, they told a story of how hard he worked and that he wasn't afraid to get them dirty. She slowly brought her eyes up when he spoke.

"Like what you see?" His lips turned up and his eyes sparkled with mischief.

Damn, he had caught her checking him out. Rolling her eyes, she answered with a huff, "I'm not here to boost your ego."

"But what if that's what I need?" He gave her those cute puppy dog eyes that no man should ever have the privilege of having access to.

"Your ego is just fine."

Was that too much sass in her voice? Probably. Was she willing to apologize for it? Absolutely not. She was sticking to the course she had set for herself. Even if it killed her.

"Ouch," he chuckled, rubbing a hand over his heart. "You sure know how to cut a guy down."

He plated their food and pushed one towards her. Shrugging her shoulders at his remark, she grabbed her fork and dug in.

"Uh," she moaned. "So good."

Turning to thank Brooks, she froze when she saw the look in his eyes. Desire. Pure and simple. He had stopped with his fork halfway to his mouth and was just watching her. No, devouring her. That's the only way she could describe the look he was giving her.

Dropping her own fork and swallowing hard, her mind completely blanked.

"Bedroom, now," he growled.

"Wha...?" She didn't get to finish her question before he was throwing her over his good shoulder. She tried to protest but barely formulated what she wanted to say before he threw her on the bed. Bouncing not once but twice, she lifted her head to protest but stopped when she saw the look in his eyes.

That heated look she had seen in the kitchen had multiplied, times ten.

"The next time you moan like that will be because my dick is pounding into your drenched pussy."

This time his voice was much deeper as if he was trying very hard to keep himself under control. No longer able to look into his piercing blue eyes, she slowly dropped her gaze to his flaring nostrils, down his neck where his Adam's apple bobbed, even lower to where his chest rose and fell like he just got done running a marathon. Everything about his body screamed he was aroused, but other than to throw her over his shoulder, he had yet to make a move.

She wasn't sure if it was a smart idea, but she brought her eyes back up to his and challenged, "So what do you plan to do about it?" She was throwing all caution to the wind and simply allowing her body to take control.

A growl deep in the back of his throat was the only warning she got before he dove at her. A squeal escaped her lips before she could stop it.

"I'm about to show you." He nipped at her collarbone, eliciting a moan. She shoved her hands in his hair and pulled him tighter, silently begging for more. Her clit vibrated with need as he ground his cock into her pelvis. The smoothness of her pants only providing a tiny bit of friction.

Frustrated, she groaned, "I need you."

He chuckled against her neck. "So damn impatient."

She bucked beneath and twisted her hips in an attempt to flip him. He must have understood what she wanted because he willingly allowed himself to be thrown onto his back.

"Yes, I am. So, I'll just take what I want."

She straddled his hips with her palms flat against his chest. The way his muscles twitched underneath her hands made her want to rip the shirt from his body. Instead, she tugged until he arched up enough to pull it free and sent it flying across the room.

The man truly had a fantastic body. He admitted he worked out but not all those muscles came just from a gym. He didn't mind hard labor and he didn't flaunt what he had. That alone made him sexier than any man she had ever had sex with.

Her eyes trailed down his chest to the V of his shorts. Her mouth watered, actually watered, at the sight of his shaft tenting his mesh shorts.

"You keep biting your lip like that and I'm not going to last long," Brooks growled beneath her.

The heated look and flared nostrils made her core vibrate. She was wet just looking at him. Sex is what she knew, unlike the feelings she was experiencing lately. She was confident in this department.

She peeled back the shorts just enough for his dick to spring free, the tip glistening with pre-come. She licked her lips in anticipation.

Scooting back off his lap, she kissed her way down from his navel to just above his erection, then back again. She continued a few more times, with each pass she kissed a little more up his length until she reached the head. Circling the tip with her tongue, she got the taste her body was craving. Torturously slow, she took all of him in her mouth. Never taking her eyes off his, she watched as they rolled back into his head.

She relaxed so she could take him deeper, letting him slam into the back of her throat. He moaned in response. Before she could continue taunting him, he was grabbing her under her arms and tossing her down onto the bed.

She whimpered. "I wasn't done yet."

"Yes, you were," he hummed. "The only place I'm finishing is right here." She groaned as he cupped her sex.

In two swift moves, he kicked off his shorts and wrestled her pants off.

"I see you're already wet for me. Good. I need you now."

He lined himself up and thrust into her. She gasped at the sudden intrusion as her nails bit into his back, pulling him closer.

He pulled out almost entirely and slammed in again, filling up every inch of her. She groaned again at how full she felt with him inside her. His fingers dug into her hip bones as he continued to slam into her over and over again.

"Yes," she gasped when he lifted her to go even deeper, her hips thrusting forward of their own accord to meet his every movement.

He was taking no mercy on her. She would be sore later, but she found she couldn't care. It was too damn good.

"I'm close. I need you with me," he grunted as his thumb massaged her nub, sending her flying over the edge.

"No condom," he gritted out. "Tell me now if you want me to pull out."

"Don't you dare," she hissed. She wanted to feel all of him. And she did. Not even a moment later, he threw his head back and roared her name as he spilled inside her.

He released her hips and collapsed forward. Wrapping him in her arms, they both took the next few moments to catch their breaths.

"Sorry I forgot a condom. I was too desperate to have you," he whispered in her ear. His forehead resting against her neck.

"It's fine. I'm on birth control and have never done it without one before."

She rubbed her hands up and down his back. He was still semi-hard inside her and slightly crushing her, but she refused to complain. She liked how close he was at the moment.

"Neither have I. This was a first for me."

His admission made her heart flutter. She liked knowing she was the first person he had shared such an intimate moment with.

When he shifted so he was resting on his elbow and slowly began pulling out, she let out a silent whimper at the loss.

"Fuck, there is nothing sexier than seeing our juices mixed together and sliding down your leg," he marveled, lightly dragging his hand across her stomach.

She expected to be grossed out by the notion, but watching the heated look return in Brooks's eyes and seeing his erection grow just moments after he pulled out of her, was enough to make her forget about how sticky it felt.

Giving him a seductive look, she panted, "I was going to clean up on my own but now I'm thinking I might need some help."

Throwing her legs over the bed, she started to saunter her way towards the bathroom. The bed shifting caught her attention just a second before the crack of him slapping her bare ass as he maneuvered around her.

"Cleaning up is my specialty."

A quick cleanup turned into multiple orgasms. The man had more stamina than she expected. The water turning to ice was the only reason they finally finished up. But that didn't stop him from reminding her what his mouth could do as well. By midafternoon she was wondering if she could even move. Not that she really cared. If she died at that moment, it would be with a smile on her face.

Chapter 25

B liss. That was the only way to describe the last couple of days with Brooks. Pure bliss. They had spent almost every moment together and not once did she wish she were somewhere else. If someone would have told her a month ago this would be how she spent her week, she would have laughed in their face.

They shared stories, discussed their favorites movies, she told him more about her favorite books, and all the while laughed more than she ever had with anyone else. Except for maybe Leslie.

All her self-doubts and worries about uprooting her life simply slipped away. So much so that yesterday she started putting a plan in motion. She booked a flight to Boston for the next day, set up a meeting with her boss, and had already contacted the manager of her apartment building to start the process of breaking her lease.

Had she told Brooks any of this? Absolutely not. Did she have a plan in place to do so? Abso-fucking-lutely. Which was why she was borrowing his truck and trying to navigate through the crazy Austin traffic.

"Wait, so you have an entire romantic evening planned?" Leslie practically squealed through the phone's speaker.

After her big ah-ha moment and a little planning, she called her best friend to share the good news.

"I mean *entire* is a strong word," she giggled. "But yeah, I guess so."

There were a few details she had left out when running through her plans. Like the fact that she planned to confess her love. That was probably the scariest thing. She had no idea how Brooks was going to respond. She really hoped it was with the same feelings, otherwise, her trip back to Boston was going to be a bit awkward. Although she had already made the decision that even if things didn't work out with Brooks, she was still moving to Texas to be closer to Leslie, and closer to her godchild.

"Oh my God, I'm going to cry. I'm so happy for you," Leslie sniffled. The baby hormones were obviously in full effect.

"Let's not get ahead of ourselves," she warned. "My luck, he won't be happy about me wanting to move down. What if I scare him off?"

She hated to sound insecure. It wasn't like her but that was all she kept thinking every time she put another piece of the puzzle into motion. What if he wasn't as ready as she was?

"Oh, please. I've seen the way he looks at you. Head over heels in love. The only person who couldn't see it was you."

Charlotte felt the heat start in her neck and slowly rise. It was a good thing Leslie couldn't see her right now. She wasn't prone to blushing but just the mention of love was having that effect on her.

"Maybe." Her response wasn't confident and the slight tremor in her voice was a dead giveaway.

"Hey, what's wrong? This uncertainty isn't like you and it's kind of freaking me out. What happened to my kickass best friend?"

She fell in love.

She wasn't prepared to say that out loud and she wasn't sure why, but something inside of her was screaming to wait until she spoke to Brooks. So instead, she pulled out her best "Charlotte is in control" voice and responded, "You're right. It's going to be great. I'm going to do a little shopping and get what I need. Then I'm going to wear an amazing dress that knocks his socks off and makes him want to tear it off me."

"That's the spirit! You go get him! I have to run but call me tomorrow and give me all the dirty details."

"You know I will," she chuckled and hung up. Feeling better after talking with Leslie, she pulled into the mall parking lot. The first thing on her list was to get something to wear. In her haste to pack, she hadn't brought anything remotely sexy, which didn't matter since all of their time had been spent chilling around the house. But for what she had planned, she really wanted something special.

Two hours later, after what felt like a million dressing room changes, she finally found the perfect dress. Since they would be eating in the backyard under the stars rather than attending someplace, she didn't want anything too fancy but still enough that he wouldn't be able to stop thinking about getting her out of it all night.

The green sundress she had chosen was exactly that and more. It made her green eyes pop. Factor in the red in her hair and she practically screamed *siren*. Only she wouldn't be luring Brooks to his death. No, she simply wanted his love and their happily ever after.

Pulling up to a red light, she jammed out to the radio. One of the many things she and Brooks had in common was their taste in music. They both preferred soft rock or nineties country. Neither of them cared for the new stuff. So when she got into his truck and found that the local station was having a nineties country marathon, she took it as a good sign.

Seeing the light turn green, she stepped on the gas and proceeded forward, screaming out, "I like it, I love it," when she was thrown sideways against the car door, her shoulder and head hitting the glass as the truck spun in circles. Gripping the steering wheel, she screamed as the scenery around her continued to spin. Moments with Brooks flashed before her eyes, and the only thing she could think about was how sorry she was that she waited to tell him how much he meant to her. The truck slowed down before teetering sideways and landing on the driver's side.

The smashed glass cut into her arm. She tried pulling herself forward, but the seat belt had her locked in place.

"Ma'am, ma'am! Are you alright?" She looked up to see a middle-aged man just outside the front windshield. While it had cracked in places, for the most part, it was still intact.

Moving her hand to wipe away some blood that had dripped down her forehead, she croaked, "I think...so."

"I've called nine-one-one, so just hang tight. Someone should be here shortly," he yelled.

At least she thought he was yelling but the ringing in her ears kept changing the pitch of the man's voice. Feeling tired, she closed her eyes and tried to lean her head back against the seat rest.

"Don't close your eyes!" he ordered. "Stay with me. I can hear the sirens now. You need to keep your eyes open!"

She could hear them as well. Slowly, she opened them back up.

"Good. Just keep them open until the paramedics show up." The man sounded relieved. She remembered reading somewhere that it wasn't good to close one's eyes after a trauma. She couldn't remember why at the moment, but she figured it was why the man kept insisting she kept them open.

The man was soon replaced by a paramedic and a firefighter who explained that they would need to cut out the front windshield to get her out. In the meantime, a paramedic would come through the back and stabilize her while also placing a blanket over her while they did the cutting. She was grateful they were explaining the process because she probably would have freaked out when someone approached her from behind and placed a collar around her neck and a blanket over her. It took only a few minutes of some really loud saw. She only knew it was a saw because the nice lady paramedic explained what was happening when she had winced, before she was rolled onto a backboard and switched to a stretcher.

Once inside the ambulance, they continued their assessment. Asking her questions about what happened and her medical history. She had no idea what happened, and fortunately for them, her medical history was easy because her head hurt too much to think.

"Is there someone we can call for you and have them meet you at the hospital?"

She looked over at the female paramedic who had been with her from the start. She was petite like herself but with dark hair pulled back into a tight bun. Her first thought was Brooks, but she couldn't remember his phone number off the top of her head.

Stupid smartphones. People weren't forced to memorize phone numbers like in the past.

After a moment she rattled off Leslie's number. It hadn't changed since college, so she knew it by heart.

They arrived at the hospital and the next hour went by in a blur. Between the testing and prodding, she began to feel like a damn science experiment. They had finally stopped and left her in peace when a commotion outside her room got her attention.

"Trust me, she will want to see me." Brooks's commanding voice couldn't be mistaken as he slammed through the door, rushing to her side.

"Charlotte! Are you okay? Leslie called me."

"Miss, are you sure it's okay? I can ask him to leave." The nice nurse looked at her with a soft smile before turning her much sterner look towards Brooks. The woman was middle-aged and reminded her of a mother bear protecting her cubs. She was prepared to toss Brooks out if Charlotte asked.

"Yes...it's okay. Thank you," she tried to reply with authority, but her voice was still a bit shaky, despite how long she had been there. With one last look, the nurse slipped back out the door. Charlotte watched the door for a beat before Brooks squeezing her hand gently got her attention.

"What happened? Leslie said you were in an accident. Why didn't you call me?" He looked genuinely hurt that it was Leslie who had to let him know what happen.

She squeezed his hand in return.

"I lost my phone, and it was her number I had memorized. Stupid technology. I only programmed your number," she explained slowly. Her head still throbbed, so talking fast hurt. "I'm so sorry about your truck."

A tear leaked out of her eye. She had this amazing night planned and now it was ruined and to top it off she had wrecked his truck. It wasn't a good way to start the relationship she wanted.

"I don't care about the truck. That can be replaced. I just care that you're okay. Did they say what happened?"

She shook her head no. The nurse had mentioned that she would need to speak with the police before she left. She didn't know when that would be.

"I'm not sure. I was going through a green light and the next thing I remember is hitting my head against the door while I spun in circles before finally falling to the side."

"She was t-boned by a driver who fled the scene."

They both looked towards the door at the newcomer.

"Abby?" Brooks was shocked to see his co-worker and friend standing in uniform just inside the doorway.

"Sorry, I asked if it was okay if I delivered the news after I heard your tags come across the radio. When they said it was only one patient, a female, I figured it might be Charlotte. Michaels was the responding officer, so he will be taking her statement. He's right outside."

"Wait, did you say the other driver fled the scene?" Brooks's voice was low and the vein on his temple was pulsing.

Abby simply nodded. Stepping back out of the door for just a moment, she returned with another uniformed officer. According to his nameplate, this was Officer Michaels.

"I'm sorry to barge in but I need a quick statement."

He looked sincere in his apology, but his eyes kept darting back and forth between her and Brooks. The officer wasn't nearly as big as Brooks, but he certainly wasn't a small man either. There was no reason for him to be concerned about Brooks except in the moment Brooks looked like a caged animal ready to strike.

"Can you tell me what you do remember?" Michaels continued.

Taking a deep breath, she thought back to the moment she was coming out of the mall.

"I had stopped at a red light leaving the mall. I was jamming to the radio"—she turned to Brooks with a smile —"'I Like It, I Love It' was playing." But he didn't return her smile. In fact, his face was in a frown. Shaking her head, she turned back to the officer. "When the light turned green, I started forward and then the next thing I know my head smashed off the door and I was spinning in circles. I don't really remember much else."

She turned to Brooks for reassurance but the look in his eyes and the tic in his jaw was anything but. She had no idea why he looked ready to commit murder. Yes, the thought of someone hitting her and fleeing the scene sucked, but just before he had said he was just happy she was okay. Was that no longer how he felt?

"We're looking for the car that hit you and fled the scene. We have a few reports from witnesses, so we'll keep you posted."

With a smile to her and a curt nod to Brooks, Officer Michaels slipped back out, leaving just the three of them. Abby had chosen to stay back.

"So they have no idea who hit her?" Brooks practically jumped down Abby's throat.

Feeling bad for the woman, she attempted to calm him down. "Brooks, I'm fine."

"No, you're not!" he shouted. "You're in a hospital bed because you were driving *my* truck. Because of *me*. You staying here wasn't a good idea."

He abruptly turned and charged out of the room like his ass was on fire, leaving a very confused Abby and tears in her eyes. A physical slap would have hurt less than those words.

How did everything get so messed up?

Chapter 26

B rooks stomped his way out of the hospital, hitting
every door with more force than was needed. His
shoulder hurt from all the extra force he was using but he
didn't care. The pain was good. He deserved the pain.
Because of him, because of something stupid he couldn't
even remember, Charlotte had gotten hurt.

Officer Michaels didn't have to tell him but what else
could it be? Less than a week after he gets shot, someone t-
bones his truck. It was clear someone wasn't satisfied he had
survived and was looking to continue to inflict more
damage. But instead of it being him, it had been Charlotte.
She had been the one driving his truck. So this was all his
fault. Stepping out into the hot summer air, he pulled his
phone out of his pocket and sent Leslie a quick text.

Brooks: She's okay and should be released by the time
you get here. Take her back to my house.

The response was almost immediate. Zack was on an
assignment, so she was either texting and driving or one of
the other girls was bringing her up.

Leslie: Where are you going? Why aren't you taking her home?

His hands flew across the keyboard.

Brooks: I need some time to think and she's safer away from me.

That was all he said before shoving the phone back in his pocket. The familiar vibration of an incoming phone call came a moment later. Ignoring it, he moved through the lot until he located the car he requested. His phone continued to vibrate over and over again. Leslie was going to be pissed but he pushed that aside for the moment. He was doing what was best.

Charlotte was in danger if she stayed here until they figured out who was behind his attack. If that meant he needed to be an asshole for a few minutes, then so be it. Her safety outweighed his need to have her with him. He should have done that from the start, then none of this would have happened. Except, then they wouldn't have had the chance for the amazing week together. One that almost felt like they were heading in the direction of a relationship.

That thought pained him. They really had been having such a good time. She had said she had a surprise for him that night and it was the reason she had gone out. He had been so happy he hadn't even thought about the threat. That was a huge mistake on his part and one he wouldn't make again. Until the individual was caught, the best place for Charlotte was away from him. Hopefully, Leslie could convince her to go visit Divot for a bit. Have some girl time.

He had the chauffer drive around aimlessly for a bit. He was running up a large tab, but he couldn't find it in himself to care. Finally, he asked to be taken to a car rental lot. He was in need of new wheels, and it was better to get it taken care of sooner rather than later. It was a couple of hours later and plenty of back-and-forth discussions with his insurance company before he was driving away in an SUV. He had wanted a truck, but one wasn't available and he couldn't do a car. He always felt crunched, and since he had to drive one for work, he avoided it as much as possible in his personal life.

Pulling out his phone he checked through the dozens of missed calls and texts from Leslie.

Leslie: What do you mean you need time to think? What the fuck does that even mean?

Leslie: Don't you dare ignore my calls. And why is she safer away from you?

Leslie: Answer me, damn it

Leslie: I'm going to kick your ass when I see you.

Leslie: If Zack wasn't away for work dealing with his own shit, I would have him come back just to knock some sense into you

Charlotte: I'm back at the house. I don't know why you're staying away. Please just come back so we can talk.

She must have gotten a new phone or someone found hers. He was tempted to go back to comfort her but then he remembered the reason he was staying away. It was safer for her. Putting his phone back in his pocket, he pushed the thoughts of Charlotte out of his mind. He needed to try and figure out who was after him and why. And he knew just the person he wanted to talk to about it.

He pulled into the precinct and pounded his way through until he found Detective Daniels's desk. He was fortunate the man wasn't out on the road. He hadn't even thought to call first. He was running on adrenaline and not thinking more than one step ahead. It was dangerous in his line of work, but at the moment he couldn't seem to find his usual calm self.

"Officer Lynch, what brings you down here?"

"Have you learned anything about who shot me? My girlfriend was involved in a hit-and-run in my truck. I'm thinking someone thought it was me," he blurted out. He had called Charlotte his girlfriend without much thought. They hadn't made anything official, but it sure felt like it.

"I'm sorry to hear that. We have a name and a BOLO out, but nothing has come in yet. You know every officer in the state is out looking. We will find him."

He did know. Two days after he was released, he had been informed that they were able to get facial recognition off his body cam. He didn't recognize the name or face when they had shown him. He still had no idea why the man had targeted him. It made no sense and he had tried to remember every call he had gone on. But after seven years, there were too many calls for him to possibly remember everything.

"I'll look into the accident, okay? See if there is any connection."

He nodded his head and walked away in a bit of a daze. He's didn't know what he expected. That the man would magically be in custody or would have turned himself in? Detective Daniels had said he would let him know the moment they had the guy and he believed him. He needed to remember that now. It was important he trusted the system. He was a piece of that system after all. Walking back to his vehicle, he drove back to his house in a fog.

He knew the moment he walked through the door that Charlotte wasn't there. The house just felt empty. Walking into his bedroom, he expected to see some of her things, but everything was gone. Since she hadn't come with much to begin with, he figured she would need everything for a stay at Leslie's. Not giving it much more thought, he snuggled up to her pillow and proceeded to quickly pass out.

Chapter 27

S he wouldn't cry anymore. She had wasted too many tears on the damn man already and she refused to continue. Begging for affection wasn't in her DNA. After he ignored the text asking him to come back and talk, she tried calling a couple of times, but he ignored those as well. So in the end, she stopped. If he wanted time to think like he told Leslie, then that was exactly what she was going to give him.

So, as planned, she was sitting in the airport waiting to catch her flight. Since last night hadn't gone as planned, she never got the chance to speak with Brooks and confess that she loved him. Instead, she was going with plan B. She had her meetings set and really the only thing that would change was instead of moving to Austin, she would be looking for places in Divot or more likely in one of the cities outside of the small town. She wasn't sure she was completely ready for the small-town life. She kind of liked having neighbors and sounds all around. The quiet of Leslie's new hometown was a bit strange for a city girl.

The new phone in her purse started ringing. Hers was smashed during the accident and Leslie had insisted she couldn't go without one. Coming from the woman who for the longest time rarely knew where her phone was, Charlotte had laughed hysterically. Zack was the reason for that change. And maybe her editor, Beth, as well. At one point Beth had threatened to staple the damn thing to Leslie's hand. She had agreed at the time. Now she wanted to burn it. That way she wasn't tempted to look at it every five minutes to see if Brooks got his head out of his ass.

Snatching it out of her purse in hopes it was Brooks, she let out a disappointed sigh.

I really should burn the fucking thing already.

"Hey."

"I take it you still haven't heard from him?" Leslie didn't even bother to return the greeting.

"That would be a negative. He wasn't kidding when he said he needed time apparently." She tried to shrug it off.

Not that Leslie could see what she was doing, but for her own peace of mind, she did. But she knew it was all an act. She had fallen head over heels for Brooks and now her heart was breaking into pieces. Exactly what she predicted would happen from the start.

"I'm seriously going to kick his ass the moment I see him. If you hadn't made me promise not to drive over there, I would have already had the pleasure of doing so."

"We can't force him. If I'm going to be with someone, then they have to want me as much as I want them. Right now that's not Brooks, and I don't know if it will ever be."

One of the many realizations she had come to last night while she cried herself to sleep was that maybe the feelings were all one-sided. She might have been the one to walk away first and then initiate the friends-only rule but at no point did he fight for her. In fact, he had easily agreed every time. So maybe it was just about sex for him. Maybe she was the one to assume he wanted more. And now she wouldn't know because her stubbornness prevented her from reaching out anymore.

"Bullshit! Do you hear me? I'm calling BULLSHIT!"

Charlotte moved the phone away from her ear. The little old lady sitting a few seats down from her looked up in shock. Giving her best apologetic look, she placed the phone back to her ear.

"There's nothing to call bullshit on. You know firsthand that he asked for this, and he has yet to answer or respond to either of us."

"That's not what I'm calling bullshit on. You might not have told me, but I know damn well you're in love with him."

There was no point in denying it. If she never spoke to Brooks again, which would be hard since they were about to be godparents together, it would break her heart, but that was for future Charlotte to worry about.

"Yes, I am, but that doesn't change anything. He has to want me. To love me back. To fight to be with me. Not run away because I got into an accident. He should have been by my side, and he wasn't."

And that was another reason why she had stopped trying to reach out to him. When she needed him the most, he had walked away. She didn't fully understand it. She wasn't sure she wanted to. What she did want was to get herself back to Boston and finish putting together her plans. Something that Trista said had sparked an idea. She hadn't thought it all the way through and there were several steps she needed to take before she could even consider moving forward on it, but she was willing to try.

"And we're back to me kicking his ass for being an insensitive jerk," Leslie huffed.

Charlotte chuckled. She couldn't have asked for a better best friend. Through thick and thin, Leslie always had her back. It didn't matter what life threw at them. And that went both ways. She would kill anyone who attempted to harm Leslie. There was still the chance that she might have to. Especially if Leslie's parents ever showed their faces again.

The announcement came on that they were beginning to board the flight. After promising to call as soon as she landed, she hung up and turned her phone off. She was removing the temptation. At least, that was what she was trying to convince herself of. She refused to turn into one of those women who checked their phone nonstop in hopes that the guy would call. She was already on that path, and she hated it. She needed to bring back kick-ass Charlotte. She was more fun.

The flight flew by despite her two-hour layover. She had been smart enough to download a few new books to her tablet. Getting lost in new book boyfriends was the perfect way to forget about the real-life ones. Brooks was never really her boyfriend, but the concept was the same.

As promised, she called Leslie once she landed. She would be lying if she said she wasn't slightly disappointed when she turned her phone back on and the only missed calls were from telemarketers. She didn't actually own a car, so she wasn't sure how she was supposed to extend the warranty on one.

She wasn't in the mood to sit in her apartment and wallow, so after dropping off what little she had and changing into something more appropriate, she decided to go to work. Michelle had taken care of her clients, and after checking in with each of them just to be sure, she was glad to know everything had gone smoothly while she was away. The new client had opted to wait until she could meet with Charlotte in person, but after a brief discussion with Trista, the woman was now willing to wait to see what Charlotte decided for a new business venture. Apparently, Trista couldn't stop bragging about Charlotte's talents and the woman wanted to see for herself and was willing to wait. That made her both excited and nervous.

"I'm surprised to see you here. I thought you were flying in today." Charlotte didn't know how she missed the click of her boss's heels. Usually, she could hear the moment Lola stepped through the door.

"I did. I just wanted to check and make sure there weren't any problems while I was gone."

Liar! You wanted a distraction and work was the only thing available.

That alone was a pathetic statement. The only thing she did besides work was read a book and talk to her best friend who moved away.

When did I get so lame?

"I assured you everything was fine. You seriously lack faith in me." Lola raised her nose in the air at the declaration.

With good reason, Charlotte thought. If she hadn't been able to leave her clients with Michelle, she would have canceled them instead. Leaving it to chance that her boss would be nice was too much of a risk. Besides, almost half of them would never have met with her anyway. Too many of them have already had their bad experience and weren't looking for a repeat.

"You said you needed to speak with me about something. I know you requested a meeting, but since you're here, you might as well get on with it."

Charlotte was never sure if her boss meant to be snippy or if it just came out naturally. There were rare times that the woman could be nice. The bored look she currently wore screamed that this wasn't going to be one of those times.

"Yes. I wanted to let you know I would be turning in my notice. I've decided to move to Texas to be closer to my godchild."

Originally she had planned to share her business idea, but seeing the mood her boss was in, she quickly rejected that idea. She had a feeling not only would she not like it but she would do something to prevent it from happening. Charlotte couldn't afford that, so she kept her mouth shut.

"Your godchild? You're leaving me, and a great position, for some whining brat?"

Considering the baby wasn't even born yet, though Lola didn't need to know that, there was no way to say the baby would be whiny. And certainly not while she was spoiling it rotten. She was going to be the fun aunt.

"Yes, that's exactly what I'm saying," she answered confidently.

She might have cared what her bitch of a boss thought before, but calling her godchild "whiny" rubbed her the wrong way. She wasn't feeling all that nice all of a sudden.

"Fine," Lola snapped. "Go. Leave now. No need for a notice. I can find a replacement easily enough. I don't need you. But," she seethed, "don't think for one second to enter the fashion world."

Holding out her hand in expectation, Charlotte pulled out her keys and dropped them into the bitch's stretched-out palm. With no words, and a smug look, she walked out the door.

There was nothing for her to grab. All of her clients were on her phone, and she kept everything backed up to files on her home computer. She wasn't an idiot. She always knew there was a possibility that she could be booted on a whim. It was why she kept a nest egg and made sure she had everything she needed at her disposal. She would never steal designs; she wasn't that type of person. However, several of the clients only stayed because of her. She would use that when the time came.

Pulling out her phone, she scrolled until she found the name she was looking for. She pressed connect and waited as the phone rang.

"Hey, lady! Got some good news for me?" Trista sounded happy.

"As a matter of fact, I do. I just walked out. I tried giving my notice, but she let me go, effective immediately," she explained.

"Don't take this the wrong way but I'm glad. You can do better than that bitch anyway, so I'm glad you finally left. Her loss. Your gain."

Charlotte chuckled. Trista wasn't one to pull any punches. It was why they instantly connected when they met. They had the same viewpoints on people and life in general.

"My gain is right. Now I just need to figure out how to break into the business. Queen bitch threatened that I better not enter the fashion world."

"Whore. She's just scared because she knows that without you, she is nothing. And let me handle your 'coming out.' You'll be so damn busy you won't know what to do with yourself."

Charlotte sure hoped so. She was completely out of her comfort zone. If it weren't for Trista's support and encouragement, she would never have even thought about this. Plus, she could really use a distraction at the moment.

"I still need someone to actually make my designs," she said with a nervous laugh. "I might be great at coming up with them but I suck at the follow-through."

"You worry too much. Once I get your name out there, you'll have dozens of people who will be stepping over each other to work for you. Queen bitch took advantage of you. She might have been a great fashion designer back in the day but it was your designs that clients were coming in for. I did my research. It was you this entire time and it should have been your name on the brand for years."

Trista's speech brought a smile to Charlotte's lips. She wasn't telling her anything new. She had known for years that her designs were being used not just by the clients but also for shows. It hadn't bothered her at the time because she never dreamed of actually becoming a fashion designer. But once Trista put the idea into her head, she hadn't been able to stop thinking about it.

"You're right," she finally admitted.

"Bitch, of course I am! Now start packing that apartment of yours up. You have a move to make!"

She burst out laughing. A couple walking by gave her a funny look but she was too busy wiping away the tears to care.

"I don't even know where I'm moving to yet!" she responded between fits of laughter. She needed a good laugh right about now.

"Don't even get me started on that sexy cop of yours. When Leslie told me what a stubborn ass he was being, I was ready to drive up there and kick his ass myself. All the girls were. With the men gone, they're all getting a little antsy."

Leslie had mentioned that the team was dealing with a difficult assignment, but she hadn't said much more than that. Whatever it was, it was clearly upsetting her best friend. It was one of the many reasons she felt bad about adding her problems to the list. Leslie didn't need the added stress during her pregnancy.

"I appreciate you all having my back but I'm good. I've survived this long without a man in my life. I won't break down. I can be just as stubborn."

Liar!

It was a good thing Trista couldn't see her expression; she was surprised her voice was as steady as it was.

"I'll wait until I see you in person to be the judge of that."

Or not. I guess I wasn't as convincing as I thought.

They talked a bit more before saying their goodbyes. Trista had arranged for movers to transport her stuff from Boston. It would be put into a storage unit until she decided exactly where she was moving. After Brooks had stormed out, she had sworn she would start looking for places, but her heart wasn't in it. Leslie had offered her a place to stay, as well as Trista and even Wes.

Zack's boss might be a grumpy man, but he would never allow her to not have a place to stay. She had been slightly intimidated the first time she met Wes. He was sexy as hell for a man who had at least ten years on her, but he wore a constant scowl and stomped around like he hated the world. Which, now that she thought about it, he might actually, considering his job. But then he smiled, and she knew instantly that whoever finally won his heart was going to be one lucky bitch. There was a softy way deep down. Way, way deep down.

Now that things were moving forward, it was time to push all thoughts of men out of her mind. Her future was waiting for her. Things were looking up.

Or so she thought. She shouldn't have counted her chickens before they hatched.

Chapter 28

B rooks was miserable. And he had no one but himself to blame. He was the one to storm out. It was his choice not to text or call Charlotte back. And it was his fault that she hadn't even tried again in a couple of days. He had said he needed this time to think and that was exactly what she was giving him.

He had quickly regretted that decision. Several times he had picked up his phone to call her and stopped himself. Torn between missing her and wanting to keep her safe. He had really thought he was making the right decision. So why did it feel so wrong?

His resolve was slowly slipping. The sleepless nights were catching up to him. He needed to at least know she was alright. But he was too much of a chickenshit to call her himself, so he settled on a different route. Pulling out his phone he hit dial and waited breathlessly while it rang.

"You have *a lot* of nerve calling me, Brooks Lynch," Leslie answered after two rings. Her voice was spitting fire, and if it were possible to be scorched through the phone, he would have been.

"I know," he added solemnly. "I'm sorry."

"It's not me you need to be apologizing to. I'm not the one you hurt with your little 'give me space' attitude and then fell off the damn planet," she scolded.

He winced at the tone. If he hadn't felt bad before he called, he sure as hell did now. Leslie had a way of cutting through the bullshit and giving it to him straight. He used to appreciate that about her, but in the present moment, it just made him feel like an asshole. He had good intentions. Or so he thought at the time. Right now, he wasn't so sure.

"You're right," he sighed. "Can you put her on so I can at least say I'm sorry to her?"

He still wanted her safe, but he owed her an explanation at least. Maybe that way, he wouldn't have fucked things up beyond repair.

"She's not here. Charlotte's back in Boston."

Leslie told him matter-of-factly. She didn't even try to soften the blow.

I guess I deserved that. But...

"Wait, she's in Boston?" He figured Charlotte would have stayed with Leslie for a bit. This whole time he thought she was only a few hours away.

"Oh, yeah. Her ass was on a plane the very next day."

The next day? What the fuck? He knew he fucked up but to leave the next day? No wonder she hadn't tried to call him. She was already back to her own life without him.

The beep for another incoming call had him pulling the phone away from his ear. Seeing Abby's name pop up, he quickly rushed out, "Hey, Leslie, I have another call I have to take."

"Fine. Whatever, but we aren't done with this conversation—" He didn't wait for her to finish before he switched over to the other call.

"Hey, Abby. Tell me you have something about the case," he greeted.

"Yes and no," she responded without any fanfare. That's what he liked about his partner. She didn't bother with fluff when it came to work. "I don't know anything about the shooting, but I got word on the hit-and-run. Turns out it was a teenager taking his father's luxury SUV out for a joy ride while his parents were away. They came back and found the damage. When they asked the kid about it, he broke down and admitted to the accident. He had been so freaked out he just drove home and parked it in the garage."

His mind couldn't process what Abby was telling him. A teenager. Not the same person as his shooter. Just a coincidence. Pushing Charlotte away had been for nothing. All the heartbreak and possibility that she might not forgive him had been for nothing. The shooter might still be out there, but it was clear the guy wasn't still targeting him.

Oh, I fucked up.

"Brooks, you still there? Did you hear what I said?" Abby sounded impatient. He had zoned out and didn't hear anything further she had said. He was too focused on the fact that he had been wrong.

"Yeah, sorry, I gotta go."

He clicked off before Abby could respond. He would have to apologize to her later, but he had another problem to fix first. Rushing into his closet he pulled out a small bag and began throwing items in. He barely noticed what he even grabbed, not caring. He had a flight to book and a plane to catch.

I'm such a fucking idiot.

The earliest flight he could get was first thing the next morning. It was probably better that way. He wanted to speak with the detective working his case and he would need to reschedule his therapy appointment. He thought about calling Charlotte rather than just showing up but immediately tossed that idea out. If he gave her warning, she would be able to avoid him, and he needed to be able to speak to her in person. Grovel at her feet.

He really wasn't a huge fan of flying. Being crammed inside a tin can never really sat well with him. However, twice he had jumped on a plane without much thought to fly to Boston. All because Charlotte was worth it. He had known that after Zack's wedding, and he should have remembered before pushing her away. Now he was behind the eight ball and trying to catch up.

Walking into her apartment building, he requested to be buzzed up. The whole time he kept praying she hadn't added him to the do-not-admit list. That would really have sucked. When the guy behind the desk told him he could go on up, he sighed in relief. Maybe she didn't hate him after all.

Getting off on her floor, just like last time, she was waiting in her doorway. Her arms folded across her chest and a scowl on her beautiful face. His heart skipped a beat and his breath caught. She always had that effect on him.

"You wasted your time coming here. A day late or a dollar short. Whatever that damn saying is," she huffed out.

If her eyes didn't give her away, he would have thought she really hated him, but he could see the sadness there. It was the driving force why he stood his ground and fought.

"I'm really, really sorry. Please just give me a few minutes to explain," he begged.

"One minute," was her only response.

"Maybe inside would be better, so your neighbors don't have to listen?"

With a roll of her eyes and a drastic sigh, she dropped her arms and motioned for him to enter. Not wasting any time, he quickly raced through the threshold and stood in her entryway. He didn't want to push his luck any further than he already was.

"Forty-five seconds."

Damn, the woman drove a hard bargain. Taking a deep breath, he said in a rush, "As I said outside, I'm really, really sorry. I thought your hit-and-run had something to do with my shooting, so I freaked out. I figured you'd be safer away from me. Although, I had thought you would go with Leslie, not all the way back to Boston, but that's another discussion entirely."

He stopped to breathe before quickly rushing on, conscious that he was almost out of time.

"I shouldn't have stormed out. Things were out of my control, and I don't like that. Coupled with the fact that I thought you were in danger, and I made some really shitty choices, so again I'll say it. I'm sorry."

"You *thought*?" She looked at him with a question in her eyes.

"I'm sorry, what?"

He had no idea what she was asking him. Clearly frustrated by the encounter, she let out her own long deep breath before slowly rephrasing.

"You said you *thought* it had to do with your shooting. Does that mean you found out it didn't?"

"Yes," he said, dragging out the word. He had a feeling where this was going. "Abby called me yesterday evening and informed me it was a teenager out joyriding with his parents' expensive SUV. He fled because he was scared, and it wasn't until his parents came home from wherever they were that they noticed the damage."

"So, let me get this straight. The only reason you're here is that you found out I'm no longer in danger. At least in your mind. If you hadn't heard from Abby, then what? You would still be in Texas ignoring me?"

And he had been right. Well, damn, when she said it like that, he really did sound like an asshole. Choosing his words carefully, he answered, "No, not just because I heard from Abby. I was already feeling like an asshole. It was why I called Leslie yesterday. I needed to apologize but then I learned you came back to Boston, and before I could get any more information, Abby had rung in and told me about the accident. It all happened at the same time."

"And yet, you never thought to reach out to me yourself? You went to Leslie first, and then when you had the information from Abby, and only after you had the news, did you finally decide to come to see me?"

Charlotte never disappointed when it came to getting straight to the point. It was confession time. If he wanted to convince her of anything, he needed to bare his soul.

"I was scared, okay? I knew I messed up walking away. It's been rough. I called Leslie first because I thought she would help me. Turns out it truly is hoes before bros. She chewed me out and I'm pretty sure will kick my ass the next time I see her."

"Yes, she will and you deserve it."

"That's fair."

He was over his one minute but not about to tell her that. The longer she allowed him to talk, the better off his chances were that she might forgive him. At least he hoped so. That, or she was already planning his murder and just waiting for the opportunity to present itself. It really could go either way with Charlotte.

"I just don't understand why you came back here so quickly," he continued. "I thought for sure you were going to stay with Leslie for a bit."

"I was coming back to Boston either way. My flight was already booked before the accident. It was part of the surprise, and one of the reasons for planning the night with you."

Wait, what? She was planning to come back anyway. That made no sense. As far as he knew, they were having a great time while she was there. Or was it only in his head?

"So, you didn't leave because of me?" He was thoroughly confused and the tone of his voice and most likely his facial expression showed that.

"No, you jerk. I love you. And I was going to tell you that night, but you stormed out. I had this whole night planned including explaining that I needed to come back to Boston so I could finalize things here before moving down. But then the accident happened, and you blew that to hell."

He had pretty much stopped listening after she said she loved him. There was something about Boston and moving but he had tuned it out. She loved him. She fucking loved him. He could jump up and down or kiss her at that moment but the look on her face stopped him. She didn't look happy to be admitting she loved him.

"You love me?" He needed to make sure he had heard that right.

"Yes, I love you, and I was willing to move to Texas to be with you," she told him sadly.

He stepped forward to wrap her in his arms, but her body language stopped him. Arms crossed, a deep scowl on her face, and she was tense. Not what he would expect from someone confessing their love for the first time.

"I love you too, Charlotte. I've loved you since that night at Zack's wedding when you walked away. You took my heart with you that night," he explained. And then it dawned on him, something else she said.

She said she *was* willing to move to Texas. Past tense.

"What do you mean you were willing to move? You would rather stay in Boston? Even though you love me?" His heart was shattering all over again.

"Yes, I said I loved you. But I didn't say I planned to let you break my heart again."

That stopped him dead in his tracks. The little bit of progress he had thought he was making quickly flew out of the window. All he could envision was Charlotte slipping out of his hands like sand. He couldn't let that happen. He was prepared to grovel.

"Does that mean you're staying in Boston?" His voice cracked, and he wasn't ashamed. He was emotional about what was happening, and he wasn't afraid to admit it.

"No, the intention was never to stay here," Charlotte explained. "I was only coming back to give my notice to my boss and break my lease. I've done that. I move in two days. Everything is pretty much packed and ready to go."

He looked around her apartment for the first time. True to her word, the apartment was packed up. There were moving boxes not ten feet away from him, but he had been too focused on her to notice them.

"Where are you moving to?" he asked, his voice thick with trepidation.

Please say Austin. Please say Austin.

He chanted in his head. He doubted that would be the case after everything that happened between them, but he could dream.

"For the time being, I plan to stay with Leslie or Trista. At least until I can find my own place in one of the cities outside of Divot."

He breathed a sigh of relief. It wasn't with him or even in Austin, but Leslie was only a couple of hours away. That was a lot better than he expected. A fuck ton better than him thinking she was staying in Boston.

"And what about us?"

He should have let it go, shouldn't have pushed the issue, but it was out before he could take it back. Now all that was left was to cross his fingers her answer was better than a "fuck off."

"I don't know. There was never really an 'us.'" Her lips turned down as she said it. "We slept together, and we were friends but we never got the chance to try a relationship. Maybe it's a sign that it was never meant to be."

He refused to believe that. He was prepared to fight this time. He had made the mistake of going along with her suggestions in the past despite how wrong it felt, but no more. This time he was fighting for her.

"No, I don't believe that, and I don't think you really do either. I'm not saying we can't take things slow, if that's what you need to trust me again, but there will be no 'just friends' anymore. Fuck that. I'm not sitting on the sidelines again. I'm fighting for what I want. For us."

His breathing was coming faster after his little speech. His pulse beating faster. He was charged up.

With eyes wide, she just stared at him, not speaking at first. If the situation weren't so serious, he would have joked that he never thought he'd see the day that he made Charlotte speechless. But it was a serious conversation, and he preferred a serious answer. Making her laugh would be counterproductive.

"You're fighting for me?" she whispered, sounding almost surprised by what he had to say. Closing the distance, he stopped when they were toe to toe. Leaning his forehead down against hers, he cradled her face with his hands.

"Yes, I'm fighting for you. Just like I should have back in April. I should never have let you walk away that night in the woods and I certainly should never have left here that first time with the bogus 'just friends' agreement. I wanted more back then but I was too afraid if I pushed, you would walk away. I'm not making that mistake again. I'm here for the long haul. No matter how long that is."

Her eyes dashed back and forth. Searching his. He poured every ounce of love he had into her gaze, baring his soul. He watched as her expression went from uncertainty to disbelief and finally to understanding. It was the last look that finally had his heart rate returning to somewhat of a normal beat.

"I still want to stay with Leslie while I get myself situated, but we can date. Like two normal people. And go from there," she whispered.

It wasn't a full commitment, but it wasn't a "no" either. He would take it. For now. He would use the time to show her this wasn't just a fling. It was forever. He messed up but he was committed to fixing every one of those mistakes.

Before he could answer, the sound of his phone ringing interrupted the moment. Tempted to ignore it, he remembered the detective promised to call. He pulled it out of his pocket, and quickly checked the display. Sure enough, it was Detective Daniels. Quickly sliding to answer, he brought the phone up to his ear with a grunt. He listened for a few minutes, too speechless to respond. By the time he hung up, the only words to leave his mouth were "thank you."

As he leaned against the wall, he continued to stare at the blank screen. "Brooks, is everything okay? Who was that?" Charlotte's concerned voice tore him out of his stupor.

"It was the detective working my case. They found the guy who shot me. He got picked up in New Mexico. They are holding him until the department can send someone to transport him back to Austin."

"That's great news. I thought you would be excited to hear that."

Her confusion was evident. He couldn't quite understand it himself. He should be excited and a part of him was. But there was still that nagging feeling that something was off. The whole incident confused him. He couldn't place the why and that bothered him. Maybe now he would get the answer and he could put it behind him.

Chapter 29

Last night had been a large mix of emotions. Between Brooks showing up and confessing his love, to deciding to give a relationship a shot, and then him finding out they caught the man responsible for shooting him, it was exhausting for sure. It had surprised her when he'd looked so lost after taking the phone call from the detective. She had no idea why he wasn't happier about the news. She had been prepared to ask him but something in his expression said he didn't understand his feelings either. So in the end, she had decided to give him time to work through it.

They had spent the evening talking about her plans for her new business adventure, and when it came time to go to bed, he had held her all night. Now she was waving him off with the promise that she would first stop in Austin for a date before heading down to Leslie's place.

Charlotte probably could have been convinced to stay in Austin, but at the end of the day, she was glad he hadn't pushed the issue. She needed to prove that her reason for moving down wasn't solely because of him. She was an independent woman after all. She loved him, and he was her world, but she would survive if he left. She refused to be one of those women who crumbled at the loss of a man.

So, she was moving forward with the original plan. She would live with Leslie and start her new business. Trista had lined up several clients who were willing to give her a shot. She had several interviews with potential employees set up for the following week and for the first time she was doing something for herself. No longer allowing someone else to use her designs to get rich. If things went well, she would be too busy to worry about if Brooks was telling her the truth. She was willing to give him a chance, but she wouldn't stop her life for him. She had made that perfectly clear.

He had seemed to understand. When he said he was willing to fight for her, she had practically swooned. It was the one thing she wanted, and she would fight for him as well. As soon as she knew he was serious. It had to be all in for both of them.

What she didn't tell him was that she had no intention of getting her own place. If he was serious about them and things moved in the right direction, then she hoped her next move would be to Austin. She already looked for shops in Austin just in case. There were a few potential places, but she wouldn't commit just yet. As always, she had a plan B. Pulling out her phone, she sent Leslie a text.

Charlotte: He just boarded the plane. I'm going to stop in Austin for the day and then I'll be headed your way.

Badass Author Bitch: Did he grovel? I hope to hell he did.

Charlotte: He did. He admitted he loved me and was willing to fight for me.

Last night Leslie had tried calling but she couldn't handle all the questions she was sure would come up. So instead, she had responded that Brooks had flown in and she would explain everything after he left.

Badass Author Bitch: It's about time he admitted it. I know what he did was an asshole move but I still hope things work out for the two of you.

Charlotte: I hope so too

Her best friend was the only person she would admit that to. The only person she would show any vulnerability to. They had been through so much that she never had to worry about what Leslie would think of her.

Badass Author Bitch: Call me later. I miss your face and I can't wait to see you again.

It had been less than a week since she had left but it felt so much longer. Especially after she decided to move. It was like when someone booked a vacation and the time spent waiting for it to come dragged on, knowing that the person would rather be someplace relaxing. Every hour she was still in Boston felt like an eternity because she knew the move was coming. It hadn't taken her nearly as long to pack as she expected. Most things she just threw in boxes.

The next day she stepped off her own plane. This time it was Brooks meeting her near the luggage carousel. She had warned him that she had tried to bring as much of her clothes with her as possible, so they wouldn't be packed away. True to his word, he was standing with all three of her very large suitcases and a huge smile on his face.

"I know we were texting, and you gave me your flight number, but I was scared you weren't really going to show," he confessed once she stood in front of him.

"I would never do that. Leslie means too much to me," she joked.

The left side of his mouth tilted up in a smile. "Of course. Wouldn't want to disappoint Leslie."

She reached for his hand and intertwined their fingers. He gave her hand a squeeze.

"You mean just as much to me," she whispered.

Fuck, when did I become so sappy?

It was Brooks. Only he could do that to her and, secretly, she loved him for it.

He framed her face with his other. Leaning her head into that hand, she relaxed completely, closing her eyes, and reveling at the moment.

"I love you, Charlotte, and I'm really happy you're here."

"I love you too, Brooks," she whispered.

"Let's get out of here. I don't have a problem with displays of affection, but I don't think the people around us would appreciate the things I want to do to you," he growled.

She giggled into his hand and placed a kiss on his palm before picking her head up.

"Indecent exposure and all that."

"Yeah, something like that," he laughed.

She would have loved to walk out holding his hand but the amount of baggage she brought prevented that. For once her over-packing actually annoyed her. They loaded everything into his rental SUV, then, grabbing her hand, he brought her around to the passenger side and opened the door for her. He waited until she was settled in her seat before planting a quick but passionate kiss on her lips. One that left her dizzy. She was grinning like a fool while he walked around the vehicle and hopped into the driver's seat, the same goofy grin on his face.

"I'm sorry I have to drop you off and run. I already rescheduled my physical therapy, and if I do so again, my therapist is likely to kill me. The last time I got the lecture about not being committed to my recovery."

He already apologized when she first told him what time her flight was coming in. At first, she had been bummed that he would be leaving so soon, even if it were only for two hours, but then she realized it gave her time to freshen up without the pressure of him watching her every move. They were still in the early stages and quickly throwing herself together wouldn't do.

"No need to apologize. I assure you I won't be bored. I have an evening to get ready for." She winked.

The heated glance he threw her told her he knew exactly what she was referring to and liked the thought. Her cheeks warmed in anticipation.

Brooks dropped her off at his house, and after helping her bring in her bags, left her with a scorching kiss. All the while, they never noticed the car lurking a few doors down.

As promised, she texted Leslie.

Charlotte: I just got to Brooks's place. He has therapy, so I'm going to spend the next two hours primping myself for tonight.

Badass Author Bitch: I'm glad you arrived safely. He better make you feel like a damn princess.

She rolled her eyes at Leslie's response. Her friend never used to be this dramatic. The baby must really be messing with her emotions. Or maybe it was because her husband was still away after a few weeks. It was his job, but Charlotte couldn't imagine it was easy not knowing what he was doing or where.

Charlotte: I'm certainly not letting him off the hook, but I won't hold it over his head either. A fresh start. That's how I'm going to look at this.

They both deserved it. She wasn't innocent in all this. He might have walked away this past time, but she had walked away first. It was a hard pill to swallow, but if she were going to blame him, then she needed to blame herself too. Instead, she decided a clean slate was the easier option. That way both of them weren't harboring any resentment. It was a mature decision. That thought made her giggle. Leslie was always the mature one of their friendship, not her.

Badass Author Bitch: Then I'm happy for you. Go rock his world and give me all the dirty details. I'm jealous.

Charlotte: How are you holding up? You avoid mentioning the fact that Zack is still gone.

She should have pushed earlier but she was so caught up in her own drama that she let Leslie change the subject often enough, but not this time. She needed to make sure her friend was okay.

Badass Author Bitch: I have the other women, so that helps. I've been helping Ash and Leah a bit with events when I'm not writing, and we all get together often enough that I'm not alone. Missy tells us what she can, but Wes is keeping her in the dark as well. If it weren't for Sophie, Ella, and Kallie, it might be boring, but those girls are such a joy.

Sophie was Leah and Arlo's daughter. She wasn't even a year old yet. Missy was the newest woman in the group. She had escaped some really bad shit and brought with her Ella and Kallie. Missy worked for Wes as the receptionist but was also dating Kyle, one of Zack's teammates.

There had been a point when she was slightly jealous of all the new friends Leslie was making, but the more time she spent visiting Leslie, the more she was happy for her best friend. It was good for her to have people in a similar situation.

Charlotte: And I'll be joining soon, so we know it's going to get really crazy. Especially since I know Trista is still in the area.

Leslie always joked that when she jumped in with Ash and Trista, the world was set on fire. It was true. The three of them were all loud and obnoxious and they fed off each other. It was great and probably exactly what Leslie needed to keep occupied.

Badass Author Bitch: Yes, Trista is still here and can't stop talking about the two of you working together. I'm so glad you finally listened to someone. I'm about to be the best-dressed author in the world.

Charlotte: Or assistant if you keep working with Ash lol.

Badass Author Bitch: She needs to hire an assistant but wants to wait until the team is back before making that move. She knows the guys will want to do a deep search on whoever she considers, so in the meantime I'm pitching in.

Ash was Bentley's girl and a kick-ass party planner. She planned Leslie's wedding and has done big events for celebrities. Another perk of having a best friend who was a model. Trista helped launch Ash's career. Similar to what she was willing to do for Charlotte. She was a generous person that way.

Charlotte: I better start getting ready. I'll call you in the morning. Love you, bestie.

Badass Author Bitch: Love you too, girly

Tossing her phone on the bed, she moved into the bathroom and turned the taps on for a bath. She had every intention of shaving her legs and soaking for a few minutes to put her in the mood. Moving back to the bedroom, she started to undress.

"Well, you're making this a little too easy," a voice she didn't recognize taunted behind her.

With a scream, she attempted to cover herself as she spun around. Just like with the voice, she didn't recognize the man standing on the other side of the room, currently between her and the door.

"Get out!" she yelled at the top of her lungs. She had no idea if there were any windows open, but she was going to try and get someone's attention if she could. She glanced down for her phone, but unfortunately, she had tossed it on the bed, closest to the door and she doubted that if she dove for it, she would reach it before the man caught her.

He only sneered at her. Noticing where her eyes shifted, he picked up the phone and smashed it on the floor, further isolating her.

"Who are you?! Why are you here?"

Her voice shook. Whether from fear or rage, she couldn't be sure. This was supposed to be a romantic night with Brooks, instead some strange man was cornering her in the bedroom and his eyes showed no mercy.

"Who am I?!" he shouted. "I'm the one whose life was ruined because your boyfriend sat back and did nothing. He killed the love of my life, and now he's going to pay."

She had no idea what he was talking about but it didn't sound anything like the man she'd come to know. Brooks would never intentionally sit back and do nothing. He loved his job and wanted to help people. It was why he became a police officer in the first place. Realization dawned on her.

"Are you the man who shot him?"

The laugh was evil and manic. Whoever this person was had clearly lost it, which probably didn't bode well for her. She needed to at least try and get away, but her situation wasn't ideal. She was only in a bra and panties but that didn't stop her from trying to dash back towards the bathroom. She would lock herself in and try to crawl out the window.

She made it to the closet door when his arms snaked around her waist. She screamed again and started flailing as he picked her up and dragged her back to the bed. Throwing her on it, she tried to sit up, but his hand shot out and connected with her face. The sting of it had her head whipping sideways and she tasted blood. She used her hand to wipe at her mouth. Her eyes burned with hatred. She refused to be one of those women who cried. She was going to fight with everything in her. Brooks would be home soon, she just needed to make it until then.

"Stupid bitch. I didn't plan to hurt you until your pathetic boyfriend showed up."

With eyes blazing, she slowly looked his way. She wasn't going to let him use her to hurt Brooks. She would rather die than be the reason he suffered.

"Go to hell," she hissed.

"Feisty. I see why he likes you so much. Too bad I don't have time for the chitchat. I have stuff to prep."

She didn't get the chance to ask him what he meant before he punched her so hard she passed out. Before she lost consciousness, her only thought was please don't let Brooks see her like this.

Chapter 30

Physical therapy was brutal, and his therapist was working him extra hard. It probably had to do with him canceling and not taking it seriously enough. He was serious about it, he had just had a busy week and now he was more focused on his evening ahead. Charlotte was at home waiting for him and absolutely nothing was going to stop them from having a romantic evening.

As if he had cursed the universe, his phone began to ring.

"What have I said about phone calls during your session?" His therapist gave him a disapproving glance.

Quickly glancing at the screen, he apologized. "Sorry, it's the detective working my case. This could be important."

He connected the call while his therapist continued to scowl at him. He gave his best apologetic smile.

"What's up, Detective?" Brooks answered, while walking to the hallway, away from the other patients.

"We have a major problem." That simple sentence stopped him dead in his tracks. "There was a mix-up and Chad Butler was released from custody last night. We just found out when we arrived to pick him up."

His head was spinning, and he thought he was going to throw up. He had a nagging feeling all morning, but he just chalked it up to being nervous that Charlotte wouldn't step off the plane. That she had changed her mind after he left.

"So, he's free and still out there?" He was having difficulties processing what Detective Daniels was saying. His emotions were all over the map and he wasn't able to focus.

"I'm afraid so. We have every officer out looking for him. As far as I know, he knew we were picking him up for the shooting, so he knows we are aware of his identity."

That got him moving again and kick-started his brain.

"Which means he could be out looking for me again."

And he wasn't home. Charlotte was. Alone. He had left her alone.

"I have to go."

He hung up before the detective could respond. Racing to his SUV, he tried calling Charlotte but her phone went straight to voicemail. He dialed again and again. By the fourth try, he knew something was wrong.

What would normally take him ten minutes only took him seven, considering he broke several laws along the way. Whipping into his driveway, he slammed on the brakes and threw the SUV into park. Shutting off the engine, he leaned over and took his gun out of the glovebox. He normally carried off duty but because he was at the airport earlier, and then his appointment, he had chosen to just leave it in the SUV. Checking the clip and chamber, he stepped out and onto the lawn. It wouldn't be smart to just barge in, so he opted to do a three-sixty around the house and see what he could observe through the windows.

It wasn't until he got to the back of the house that he saw Charlotte. Looking through the back door, he could see straight into his living room. Charlotte was strapped to a chair in just her bra and panties. The man from his body cam, the one Detective Daniels had said was Chad Butler, was standing over her, facing the front door as if he was waiting for Brooks to enter. There was a good chance he had heard him arrive. Pulling out his phone, he dialed Detective Daniels.

"He—" He didn't let the man finish before he cut in.

"I found him. He's inside my house and has Charlotte strapped to a chair. I'm going in."

Brooks heard mumbling but couldn't make out the words. It was likely Detective Daniels was talking to his partner. "We're calling it in. Don't enter until backup arrives."

He didn't bother to answer with more than a grunt before hanging up. He refused to make a promise he most likely wasn't going to be able to keep. There was no way he was going to wait for anyone when he was this close to Charlotte and that maniac. He would never be able to live with himself if something happened to her.

Reaching down, he tested the sliding glass door; it was unlocked. He slowly began to open it. Raising his gun, he entered his house.

"It's about time you showed up."

Chad Butler was twenty-five years old with shaggy black hair and stubble around his chin. He wasn't fat but it was clear he had let himself go since his license picture was taken. After they had identified his shooter, Brooks had made sure to learn what he could about the man, including checking out his social media pages. Unfortunately, about a year ago he had stopped posting and had pretty much gone off the grid and everything before that was a lot of pictures of scenery and places the man had visited.

"Yes, I'm here. So you can let her go. This is between the two of us. She has nothing to do with it."

He looked over to check on Charlotte, but she was out cold. For a moment he thought she was dead, but he could see her chest rising and falling. Knowing she was alive but strapped to a chair did nothing to stop his blood from boiling. Her head was slumped away from him but he thought he saw a red mark on her beautiful porcelain skin and swelling near her lip and eye but he couldn't be sure. The thought had his nostrils flaring and his blood pressure rising.

How dare he touch what is mine?

An evil laugh brought his focus back to the unhinged intruder who was waving a gun around with no clear regard for safety.

"It has everything to do with her. You took the love of my life from me, so now I'm going to take her from you."

He was thoroughly confused. He had no idea what Chad was referring to. From all reports, the man didn't have a girlfriend now or in the past. From the few people Detective Daniels had spoken to, the man was shy and quiet and never had a serious relationship that they were aware of.

"You're going to have to catch me up. I can't help you until I know who you're talking about," he tried to reason.

"Of course, you don't remember her. She was just a blip on your radar. You went right back to your perfect little life," the man spat out. Pacing back and forth, clearly agitated with how the discussion was going so far.

"You're right. That was wrong of me, so how about you help me remember?" He needed to keep the man calm until backup could arrive. He thought he heard sirens in the distance a few seconds ago and possibly cars on the street, but he refused to look. The longer he kept Chad focused on him, the better off he was. That way his co-workers could do their job.

"You wanna remember?!" the man shouted. "Does the name Jennifer Schultz ring a bell?!"

He physically flinched at the name. He remembered it well. It was one of the worst calls he had in a while, but that didn't make any sense. She didn't have a boyfriend. He had spoken with her parents extensively after the accident and not once did they mention a boyfriend. In fact, they had said how free and wild she had been. Enjoying her youth. It was why it had hit him so hard.

"I see you do remember her," Chad laughed humorlessly. "So you remember standing by and doing nothing as she died under that truck?"

Brooks remembered every detail, but Chad had it wrong. Jennifer hadn't been paying attention when she crashed into a tractor-trailer. The top of her car was cut clearly off, severing her spine. The coroner had confirmed she was dead upon impact. He had been the first on the scene and had tried crawling into the car to check for a pulse, but it was no use. He could tell by the angle of her head she was dead. It was confirmed moments later when the paramedics joined him on the scene. There was nothing he could do for her.

So yes, he stood by as they loaded her up. He had contacted her parents and broke the news. He had stayed there long past his shift as they told him all about their daughter and what a happy child she was. Then, he had gone home and cried. He wasn't ashamed about it. The loss of a young life had hit him hard.

"You got your information wrong," he tried to reason. "There was nothing I could do. She was dead on impact. The coroner confirmed it."

"No, no, no!" Chad screamed. "I would have felt it when she died. We were soulmates. You left her to suffer in that car by herself, taking hours to finally get her out."

Brooks flashed back to that night—the flashing red and blue lights of the police cars, fire trucks, and ambulances, standing by as it took the firefighters a while to extract the car from underneath the tractor-trailer. Jennifer had hit it with such force that not only was the top of her car sliced off, but the trailer was actually on top of the car and mangled together. He had been lucky to slide in enough to get a visual on her. By the time the firefighters stabilized the trailer and were able to pull the car free, it had seemed like an eternity, and all the while, a poor girl's lifeless body lay in the driver's seat.

"Yes, it took a while to get her out but she was already gone," he murmured. His own guilt was threatening to choke him.

It had taken weeks to get over the fact that there was nothing he could have done differently to save her. For the first time in his life, he spoke with the department shrink and she had confirmed what everyone had told him. It was the autopsy report that finally helped him see everyone was right. It didn't matter if he had shown up a minute earlier or was even there when it happened. She was dead as soon as her car hit.

Shaking himself out of the spiral he was falling into, he looked again to Charlotte. Letting her presence calm him and bring him back to the present. It was important that he stayed focused. For Charlotte's sake.

She had yet to move, and if he couldn't see she was still breathing, he would have been worried he was losing her. Whatever Chad had done had knocked her out good. He hoped he wasn't risking permanent damage by drawing this out, but he didn't see any other solution at the moment. Chad was too much of an unknown. Anything could set him off and he could start shooting. While he was confident that the team outside could handle it, he wouldn't chance Charlotte getting hurt in the crossfire.

"You're just saying that to make yourself feel better!" Chad sobbed. "You don't want to admit that you fucked up. That your delay was the reason a vibrant young woman died well before she should have. We were supposed to have a life together. Get married and have children. But now that's all gone because you refused to do anything! You refused to help her!"

Chad was growing more hysterical the longer he spoke, his actions becoming more erratic. He was swinging the gun between Brooks, Charlotte, the ceiling, and every direction in between.

"Maybe you need some motivation to finally admit the mistakes you made." Chad stepped toward Charlotte and grabbed her by the hair. She whimpered but didn't open her eyes. He was grateful she wasn't able to see what was happening.

"You're right." He stepped into line with Chad. "I made a mistake and needed to be reminded." Chad had moved so that his profile was in direct line with the window. Brooks saw the red dot that appeared. It was important he kept Chad right where he was. And make sure that the man didn't realize they weren't the only ones here.

"You're damn right you needed the reminder. Maybe watching your girlfriend die in front of you would help."

A lot of things happened at once. Chad moved the gun in the direction of Charlotte's body. Brooks lunged forward, screaming no, just as he heard the glass breaking and saw Chad's body jerking. Blood sprayed all over him as he tackled Charlotte, cradling her head as they hit the ground. He didn't move as the screaming officers cleared the house around them.

"Come on, Charlotte. Wake up for me, beautiful," he whispered harshly, moving the hair from her face. She did indeed have a red mark on her cheek and both her lip and eye were swollen from where Chad must have struck her.

"Please wake up, beautiful. I can't lose you. I love you too much."

Tears streamed from his eyes, but he no longer cared. He needed Charlotte to wake up. For her to open her gorgeous eyes and sass him. He would give anything to hear a snarky remark at the moment.

"Charlotte, please," he begged.

"Brooks," she groaned barely above a whisper. The air from his lungs whooshed out at the simple word. He peppered her face with kisses, careful to avoid the injured areas.

"I'm here, beautiful. Open your eyes for me."

He needed to make sure she was awake and not just mumbling while still out; she looked to have been knocked around pretty hard. The rage coursing through his veins threatened to take over but he tamped it down. The last thing she needed was to wake up and see anger in his eyes. Fixing his features, he continued to stroke her cheek when her eyes began to flutter open. She struggled with the one that was swollen but the sight of her bright green eyes was all he needed to relax, just a little bit.

"You're bleeding." Her voice was hoarse, and he had to lean in to hear what she said.

"It's not mine," he admitted. Her only response was an O-shaped mouth. "It's going to be okay. I got you. I love you so much and I'm never letting you go."

Chapter 31

It had been a week since he walked into his house and found Charlotte tied to a chair. A whole week since he had thought he was going to lose the best part of his life. That night was supposed to be their real first date, and instead, they had spent the evening in the hospital. It turned out Charlotte did have a concussion, but other than the marks and swelling on her face, she hadn't been hurt in any other way. Chad had broken into his house and caught her by surprise as she was getting ready to take a bath. It explained the bra and panties. Relief poured out of him when he learned the man hadn't attempted to touch her.

He had stayed with her that night in the hospital after he got looked at himself. He had fallen on his already injured shoulder, and they were worried he tore something. Fortunately for him, he didn't do any extra damage, but his physical therapist was clearly not happy that he stormed out without a word and then put himself in a situation that could have reversed all the hard work.

Detective Daniels had stopped in and explained what they learned about Chad. Turns out the man had never even met Jennifer. He had cyber-stalked her for months through her social media accounts. He lived in an apartment alone, and when they went to his place, they found hundreds of photos printed off from her accounts, including those posted after she passed away. They also found several news articles from the accident. From the looks of it, Chad had obsessed over her death and blamed Brooks for it after seeing a picture in the paper of him, standing off to the side while the fire department attempted to stabilize the trailer. He never even knew the article existed. He had been in such a bad place after the call that he couldn't look at anything to do with it.

Charlotte had asked about Chad since she was out of it during the entire exchange. At first, he had wanted to shelter her from the details, but Leslie had reminded him that if he wanted Charlotte to trust him, then he needed to open up. So that was exactly what he did. He told her about the call itself, how powerless he felt when there was nothing he could do to save the life of the young woman who was already dead when he arrived. He talked about the spiral he had gone through afterward and the people he talked to, to work through the problem. And then he explained everything he had learned about Chad. The reason the man blamed him and how he twisted the situation until he thought he was avenging the woman he was secretly in love with.

Charlotte had cried with him. First for the woman who had lost her life, and then for him. The accident had been before Zack's wedding, before they had gotten to know each other. Maybe if he had her at the time, he wouldn't have spiraled as fast. He would have had someone to talk to about it before shutting down. But now he had her. Even if she was living with his brother at the moment.

Sitting on his brother's couch, he watched as Charlotte wore a hole into the living room floor. "I'm meeting with Trista today and the lawyer. We are getting the paperwork together for the business. I can't believe it's all happening so fast." She had a deer-in-headlights look. Her face had finally healed. The swelling had gone done within a few days.

As planned, Charlotte was starting her own business. She was breaking into the fashion world despite what her old boss had said. In anticipation of retribution, she was meeting with a lawyer and having everything settled just in case. His girlfriend, yeah, they were dating now officially, wasn't afraid of a fight but she also didn't want to start her business adventure with problems. So this was just one of many steps she was taking to ensure it was a smooth transition. He was so proud of her.

"Trista doesn't strike me as the type of person who waits around. Once she has an idea in her head, she pushes forward full force." He didn't know the model well, but after meeting her it was clear to see why she was so successful. "No" wasn't something the woman accepted.

"You got that right." Leslie joined them in her living room, followed by his brother. Zack had just gotten back from a pretty tough assignment, and it was clear that he was still struggling with whatever happened. He'd offered to speak with him, but Zack had waved him off. If it weren't for Leslie ensuring him that the team was handling it together and all of them were speaking with Kyle's therapist, he would have pushed. But he decided to watch instead. If at any point it seemed like what Zack was doing wasn't working, he would step up and help his little brother.

"I'm not sure why you're so nervous. Your designs are kick-ass and you already have a client list a mile long," Leslie added.

"Exactly," Charlotte screeched, actually screeched, as in her voice went up ten octaves higher than normal. He hadn't even known it was possible. "I don't want to disappoint them and what if I can't keep up?"

She was starting to hyperventilate. His strong, confident woman was actually legit nervous.

Walking over he wrapped her up in his arms and rubbed her back. It took her all of two seconds to bury her face into his chest and cling to him as if she was drowning.

"I have faith in you. So does Leslie, Zack, Trista, and a whole slew of other people who adore you. They aren't going to let you get behind on anything. Just be yourself. You're a natural," he comforted her.

Leslie joined them and wrapped her own small arms around the two of them. Burrowing her head in until she was face-to-face with her best friend.

"Brooks is right. You're going to rock this because I know you have it in you. And no matter what, we're here for you."

Charlotte sniffled but he could also feel her lips turn up in a smile against his chest. Leslie had the magic touch. He had always known that but he got to experience it firsthand this past week. He had chosen to stay with her rather than going back home. He couldn't bear to go back to his house yet anyway. He wasn't sure he ever would. They hadn't talked about it but he planned to get Charlotte's opinion before deciding where to live. He had a few more weeks of physical therapy before he could start working again.

The question was, would he go back to his life in Austin or start fresh somewhere else? He couldn't see himself as anything but a police officer and he still had aspirations of being a SWAT officer.

"I have the best people in my life," Charlotte breathed out.

"Of course, we're the best," Leslie huffed.

Charlotte burst into laughter, playfully smacking her best friend. "Shut up. That wasn't meant to give you a big head."

"Why? You already have one. I'm just catching up!" Leslie laughed as she danced away from Charlotte's second attempt at swatting her. The rest of them joined in; it felt good to have them all laughing again. Even Zack seemed sincere about it. Maybe he would be okay after all.

"Besides, the sooner you start, the sooner we can celebrate," Leslie added. "And make an announcement," she attempted to casually throw out under her breath. But Charlotte wasn't having it.

"Wait, you got the results?!" Charlotte shouted. "And you didn't tell me?!" She was even louder than before.

"There was a lot going on and you were busy. You and Brooks haven't exactly been socializing much the past few days," his sister-in-law grumbled.

It was true. He didn't really care that he was staying with his brother. He and Charlotte had some catching up to do and a lot of that time was spent in the guest bedroom. Or out on dates. He wasn't ashamed, and based on the smug look on Charlotte's face, neither was she.

"You wouldn't be socializing either if you were finally getting steady cock," Charlotte sassed her best friend. "Oh wait, you are and you've done the same thing in the past!"

His girlfriend didn't bother pulling punches.

"La la la la la. I don't want to hear about my brother's cock." Zack closed his eyes and stuck his fingers in his ears like a toddler. Leslie merely chuckled at the scene.

Pulling Charlotte in for a sideways hug, he whispered into her ear, "You can talk about my dick anytime, beautiful."

She slapped his stomach but chuckled as she buried her face in his chest. His heart swelled at the sound. He had been concerned after the Chad incident that she would have some lingering effects, but not his Charlotte. She had cursed him sideways and then promptly forgotten the man existed. He wasn't sure it was the best coping mechanism, but as he was doing with Zack, he was watching Charlotte carefully. If at any point it looked like it was indeed causing her harm, he would swoop in and fix the problem.

"I better get going before I'm late. Don't think I forgot about the bomb you dropped." She turned and pointed at her best friend. "You better have plans to share that news soon. I want to know what my little godchild is so I can start spoiling them now."

"I will, I promise." Leslie rolled her eyes.

He walked Charlotte out to her new SUV. Now that she was in Texas, it was important she had her own vehicle. She had protested at first, but after a couple days she realized there was no way she could depend on someone else driving her around. Especially not in the small town of Divot. He had laughed when she had practically stomped into the car dealership, expressing her unhappiness. That was until she got to pick out the vehicle she wanted. Now she wanted to drive everywhere. Apparently, she enjoyed her newfound freedom. He had also finally gotten a new truck. It had taken some time for the insurance to come through.

He waved as Charlotte drove off. While she was busy with moving forward with her new business, he had plans for their future. He had promised to move at her pace but that didn't mean he wasn't going to be prepared. He wanted a ring to slide on her finger the moment she was ready for a commitment because he already knew what his future held. He had seen it while he was lying in the hospital bed after getting shot. It was just a matter of Charlotte catching up to him.

Chapter 32

S he'd done it. Over the past three days, she had attended meetings and appointments. She'd had several near panic attacks; each one she was helped through by her best friend or the love of her life. It was still shocking to think she actually had that. Not the best friend part of course, but the love of her life. She had thought it would be a cold day in hell before she let someone into her heart like that. She was happy to admit she had been wrong.

Everything about her time with Brooks over the past week and a half had been nothing shy of amazing. She didn't know she could become so close to someone who still let her be herself. A small part of her had expected he would want a trophy wife, like her mother had been, but no. He supported every decision she made. He cheered her on. And not once did he try to make a decision for her. He had every confidence in her. And because of it, she fell deeper in love each day.

"So how much longer until you can go back to work?" she asked as she slipped into a pink dress. Today, they were headed to Wes's place for a party. What people didn't know was Leslie and Zack planned to announce the gender of the baby. She was voting girl, hence the pink dress.

"Trying to get rid of me already," he joked. Sliding up behind her and snatching her waist as he nuzzled her neck. She giggled while tilting her head to allow him better access.

"No, hot stuff." She pretended to sound annoyed but only managed to laugh when he licked her collarbone. "I just see how anxious you're getting lately."

"So maybe you need to keep me occupied."

Her only response was to snort. Every waking minute she wasn't busy with the business, she was wrapped around him. The man was insatiable, like he needed to make up for the months they were just friends.

"I'm pretty sure I keep you plenty occupied."

He twisted her until she was facing him. Their foreheads touching. "You're right, beautiful, you do. But for some reason, I can't get enough of you. It's like my body is starved and only you can give it what it needs to survive."

She melted into him. How she had lucked out with this man she would never know. He was rough and demanding in bed, but then he would say stuff like that and completely fall in love with him all over again.

"I know what you mean."

Her arms snaked around his back as she leaned her head into his chest so she could listen to his heartbeat. Sex used to be just that. Sex. A means to an end. But with Brooks, it was a connection. A way for the two of them to show each other how they felt without words.

"How mad do you think Leslie would be if we showed up late?" he whispered above her head.

She stepped back and swatted at his chest. "We absolutely will not be late to the announcement of our godchild's gender."

He roared with laughter. Grabbing her hand, he attempted to pull her back in but she halted his advancement. "I'm kidding!" He continued to laugh.

She side-eyed him but finally let him pull her in. "I would never make us late. Pregnant Leslie scares me too much."

Now that made her laugh hysterically, knowing it was true. She couldn't believe the change in her friend. Leslie hadn't been meek since college, but she certainly wasn't as vocal as she had become since marrying Zack. She no longer censored herself.

"And speaking of, we better get going. But first I must say, damn, you look beautiful in that dress."

A smile from ear to ear broke out across her face. She wasn't a vain person; she took care of herself enough to know she wasn't a hag. But she always truly felt it when Brooks complimented her.

"You don't look so bad yourself, hot stuff." She winked.

It was an understatement. Even in jeans and a polo, he made her mouth water. His damn clothes hugged him in all the right places and showed off every amazing quality he had. It was no wonder she had a hard time keeping her hands to herself. The damn man oozed sex appeal.

"We better leave before I do something about that look you're giving me. You're testing my damn patience."

She only smirked as he followed her down the stairs and out to his truck. Opening the door for her and giving her a hand to climb in, she leaned down to whisper, "I could ditch the panties for the day and give you something to look forward to?"

His fingers snaked out and flicked her sex, and with a moan she let her head fall back.

"Looks like we will be finding our special spot in the woods today after all," he sassed.

He plopped a kiss on her chin, swung her legs in, and slammed the door before she had a chance to respond. Damn the man for being better at teasing her. She hadn't expected that response, but she should have. He was the only person who challenged her more than she challenged him.

The drive to Wes's took barely five minutes. In a town this small, with essentially no traffic, every commute was quick. She wasn't sure she liked it. It was almost eerie how close everyone was to each other.

As with every time before, Wes's place was stunning. Not because it was done up but because of the natural beauty. There was no way to diminish it, and every time Wes added another element, it only intensified the raw look. Whenever the stubborn man found a woman, she was going to be one lucky bitch.

"I don't care where we choose to live but I need to model any backyard after this," Brooks said in awe.

"You won't get a complaint out of me."

They hadn't talked much about their future other than to confirm they planned for it to be together. She knew they would need to discuss where they planned to live but the timing never felt right. She didn't want to burst their happy bubble with logistics. Especially since she really didn't want to go back to his house. She would live anywhere else with him, but she couldn't stomach the thought of living in a house where the man who shot him, and later tied her up, had died.

"Does that mean you're ready to live with me?" he asked hopefully.

Turning completely to the side in her seat, she locked eyes with him. "I thought I made it clear my future was with you."

"You did. I just wasn't sure that meant you were ready to start house hunting."

"House hunting?"

"You didn't really think I would move us back to my place after everything that happened there, did you?" He raised an eyebrow to further emphasize his point.

"Oh, thank God"—she threw herself forward at him—"I was really hoping that's how you felt."

He chuckled at her dramatics. When she wanted to, she could ramp up her emotions and put them on full display. Right now was one of those times. She really wanted him to see how she truly felt about the situation.

A loud rapping on her window made her jump. Turning around with a scowl on her face, she met a smirking Zack. She didn't get the chance to reach for the handle before he yanked the door open.

"You two lovebirds going to come out at some point? My wife is getting impatient."

"Leslie is or you are?" Brooks challenged.

"It's one in the same these days," Zack replied. "Now come on!"

He grabbed her hand and dragged her out of her seat. Looking back, she rolled her eyes at Brooks. His only response was to chuckle. There was no point in fighting Zack when he was in his current mood. He wouldn't stop until he got his way.

She waved to her friends as Zack continued to drag her along, everyone giggling as they watched the pair. No one was surprised by the way the father-to-be was acting. As much as Leslie tried to keep it under wraps that she was announcing the gender today, she knew better. You didn't keep secrets amongst this group. The men sniffed it out and the women were just that in tuned to each other.

"Can I have everyone's attention?" Zack yelled the moment they stepped onto the patio. "Yo, fuckers, stop talking and pay attention to me."

"It's hard not to when you don't shut up," Wes boomed, causing another round of laughter.

Charlotte was so glad Leslie had found this group, and by extension, so had she. Leslie replaced her on the patio and now she was firmly tucked back into Brooks's side.

"Is your family going to be upset they weren't here for the announcement?" She was surprised they weren't here; they had a tight family.

"Zack video chatted with all of them this morning. We are actually the last ones to find out," Brooks answered.

Well, damn. She wasn't sure if that tidbit made her sad people knew before her or glad that she was finding out in person. Before she could dwell on it, Zack was shouting again.

"Drumroll, please!" The man actually made drum noises loud enough to wake the dead. "Baby Lynch is a..." Flipping up his own shirt, he exposed a custom shirt with the ultrasound photo with the baby holding a rifle, and in big letters: "A Damn Boy, Bitches."

"That's right, a little boy! Just like I said, so pay up, assholes."

There were tons of hoots and hollers, lot of giggling at Zack's overdramatic reveal and congratulations all around. The huge smile on her friend's face was enough to take the sting out of the baby not being a girl. Making her way to Leslie, she wrapped her in a hug.

"I'm so happy for you! But you're going to have to have more kids, so I get at least one little girl," she giggled.

"I don't think you're going to be too far behind me in the baby-making department."

Leslie tossed a look over her shoulder with a wink to Brooks, who was standing with his chest pressed to her back. She smirked as she followed her friend's gaze and crashed into Brooks's heated stare. The thought of kids used to scare her, but not anymore. Since those children would be with him.

"You're probably right," she admitted with a smile.

Brooks's gaze went from heated to molten in a flash. Spinning her around he cupped her ass so she could feel his erection.

"You want to have babies with me," he growled, not really a question but she nodded yes anyway. "Lots of babies," he continued, his voice got deeper.

She chuckled. "Let's start with one and go from there."

He let out a triumphant hoot as he tossed her over his shoulder, smacking her ass.

"Where the fuck do you think you're taking me, you damn caveman?" She tried to sound exasperated, but it only came out breathy. She was too turned on to give him any sass.

"To our spot. I fully plan to start the baby-trying process immediately."

The hoots and hollers couldn't be missed. She should have been embarrassed. Any normal woman would have been by the declaration in front of everyone, but not her. She was too damn excited that he had practically claimed her in front of everyone. He had fought for her just like he said he would. No, instead of being embarrassed, her face only showed how happy she truly was.

Epilogue

One Month Later

He and Charlotte stood outside their new house. They had started looking just days after Zack and Leslie announced they were having a boy. As much as rooming with his brother was fun sometimes, they needed their own space. Especially if they planned to continue their efforts to have a baby. Once the idea took root in Charlotte's head that there was the possibility of cousins growing up together, she was all on board. He certainly wasn't going to complain about the enthusiasm.

Which led them to their current situation. They signed the paperwork for the house yesterday and today was move-in day. Well, sorta. Charlotte had decided they needed all new furniture for their life together, so "move in" meant they watched as piece after piece of furniture was being delivered.

"Do you think you got a big enough fucking house?" Zack threw out as he walked by with boxes stacked in his arms. "I mean really, five bedrooms? How many kids do you plan on having? Ten?"

"Ten?!" Charlotte shrieked. "No fucking way this body is popping ten kids out."

Brooks chuckled as he looked at their new house. It did have five bedrooms and was located in a newer development, the kind where most homes were almost cookie cutter. He thought at first he would hate it, but the neighbors were friendly and so far the HOA hadn't pissed him off, so he figured they were off to a great start.

"He's kidding," he reassured her. "Besides, I wouldn't force our kids to share a room. I did that and my brothers were such a pain."

"Ain't that the truth," Garrett grumbled as he, too, walked by with boxes.

His parents had offered to help them get the house put together and dragged Garrett along. Of course, Leslie wouldn't miss out, and where she went, Zack was. Rhett was still deployed, and no one had heard from Alexa in a few days. That would normally worry a family, but she did it so often that they were used to it. She knew if it were less than a week, they wouldn't send out a search team, so she had two more days to reach out to someone. Lucy was acting strange, so he wasn't surprised that she hadn't shown. She had been busier than usual lately. His mother was giving her another couple of months before she declared an intervention. He wasn't so sure he was willing to wait that long. It was obvious something was up with his older sister.

"I don't need ten from you, sweetheart." His mother stopped next to Charlotte. "I'd be happy with two or three from each of you." A smile lit up her face. His mother couldn't contain the excitement that not only one, but now two, of her sons were even discussing the possibility of grandbabies for her.

"I can do two." Charlotte nodded enthusiastically.

He had yet to convince her for more than that. She'd eagerly agreed to two because, as an only child, she understood how lonely life could be, but she had choked at the thought of more. He would do his best to convince her, but really, he was fine if they only had two. That was what he had seen for his future, and he saw how happy he was. There was no reason to push it.

"She says that now but that's only because you're in the fun stage of simply having a shit ton of sex," Leslie added as she joined them.

His sister-in-law was just barely starting to show with the cutest little baby bump. After Zack's obnoxious announcement, it was almost like their little boy decided it was time to make his presence known. Which only made the father-to-be that much more of an obnoxious asshole. One would swear he was the first man to knock up his wife with a son the way he was carrying on. Brooks was starting to feel bad for Leslie.

"You're the happiest pregnant person I have ever seen." Charlotte gave her friend the funniest look.

"That's probably the most ridiculous thing I have ever heard you say, considering you barely know any pregnant women."

The looks exchanged between the two best friends were almost comical. Leslie's was practically a "what the fuck" look and Charlotte almost looked constipated with how hard she was concentrating. Not that he would tell her that. He valued his life and especially his balls.

"You know what, you're right. But you're still the happiest person I know, so there's that." Charlotte stuck her tongue out. The rest of them laughed at the exchange. He couldn't be happier.

His life was exactly how he hoped it would be. Almost. He was finally back to work, but unfortunately, his injury meant he hadn't been able to finish the SWAT testing. But he was still hopeful. He planned to use the time between now and the next offering to strengthen his shoulder. He wasn't back to one hundred percent, but with hard work, he could be. And even if he never made SWAT, he knew his future was still bright. He had other options. As long as he continued in a line of work that helped others, he would be happy with what he was doing.

As for Charlotte, her business venture was starting out successfully. She rented a building in downtown Austin, and she had employees starting this week. Tonight, they were going out to celebrate her success, and hopefully, add another celebration to the mix.

He thought back to the ring Leslie had helped him pick out a few weeks ago. He had been holding out until the right time, but he couldn't wait any longer. They had a new home, were already trying for kids, hell, she could already be pregnant for all he knew, and she had started her business. Life was good.

"What has you thinking so hard?" Charlotte slid up and wrapped her arms around his middle.

"You. Our future. And how happy it all makes me," he admitted shamelessly.

"I can't wait to see what our future holds."

"Me too, beautiful. Me too. I love you," he said as he brushed his lips against hers.

"I love you too, hot stuff."

Check out the next book in the
series, Burning for Chloe, featuring
Garrett.

Interested in reading about Zack
and his teammates?
Check them out in my Charlie
Team Series.

Where to find me

Interested in staying in touch?
I love connecting with my readers.
For sneak peeks, teasers, and a fun community
please join Elizabella's Ladies Reader Group
or follow me on Instagram and TikTok

Acknowledgments

Thank you Rita for always reading my work in it's rawest form. Thank you to my tribe and readers who have supported me from the beginning. My team is slowly growing but I'll never forget the originals! Thank you Rosie for putting up with my crazy schedule. I know I'm always sending you a curveball or two!

Also By Elizabella Baker

Charlie Team Series:

Ashlynn's Savior

Leah's Warrior

Zack's Redemption

Missy's Champion

Jaime's Vengeance

Heroes of Lone Star Series:

Fighting for Charlotte

Burning for Chloe

Coming Soon:

Westley (February 2022)

Bravo Team Series- Releasing 2022

Made in the USA
Middletown, DE
12 July 2022

69083167R00154